MW01045439

Sally Rippin

CHENXI

AND

THE FOREIGNER

wai (outside)

guo (country)

ren (person)

SALLY RIPPIN

CHENXI
AND ★ THE
FOREIGNER

annick press
toronto + new york + vancouver

© 2009 Sally Rippin

Annick Press Ltd.
All rights reserved. No part of this work covered by the copyrights hereon may be reproduced or used in any form or by any means—graphic, electronic, or mechanical—without prior written permission of the publisher.

First published 2008 by Text Publishing, Melbourne, Australia

Copy edited by Pam Robertson
Proofread by Tanya Trafford
Cover and interior design by Irvin Cheung / iCheung Design, inc.
Cover photograph: Irvin Cheung / iCheung Design, inc.
Cover model: Anna Warshawski

Cataloguing in Publication
Rippin, Sally
        Chenxi and the foreigner / Sally Rippin.

ISBN 978-1-55451-172-3 (pbk.).—ISBN 978-1-55451-173-0 (bound)

        1. China—History—Tiananmen Square Incident, 1989—Juvenile fiction.
I. Title.
PZ7.R486Che 2008   j823   C2008-907004-6

Printed and bound in Canada.

Published in the U.S.A. by:	**Distributed in Canada by:**	**Distributed in the U.S.A. by:**
Annick Press (U.S.) Ltd.	Firefly Books Ltd.	Firefly Books (U.S.) Inc.
	66 Leek Crescent	P.O. Box 1338
	Richmond Hill, ON	Ellicott Station
	L4B 1H1	Buffalo, NY 14205

Visit our website at **www.annickpress.com**

To Chenxi

"Love is of all passions the strongest, for it attacks simultaneously the head, the heart, and the senses."

—Lao Tzu (600–531 BCE)

CONTENTS

INTRODUCTION

When I arrived in Shanghai in 1989 as a pale-skinned, blue-eyed Australian, I was stared at and followed wherever I went. Many Chinese had never seen an outsider before, and I was treated with great curiosity, and sometimes suspicion.

China has always had an uneasy relationship with the West, and throughout the 1960s and 1970s most foreigners were banned from entering the country. Under the rule of Mao Zedong, the leader of the Communist Party, the Chinese people endured turbulent times, from extreme famine to the devastating effects of Mao's Cultural Revolution. During this period intellectuals, artists, and anyone considered to be anti-communist or to have an association with the bourgeois views of the West were denounced and imprisoned or killed. Hundreds of thousands of people were sent to the countryside to work in farms, and entire cities collapsed into anarchy. Unknown to the West, over the years that Mao ruled China behind closed doors, millions of people were victimized and killed.

China remained closed to foreigners until Mao Zedong died in 1976. In the next decade, the new leader of the Communist Party, Deng Xiaoping, began a series of economic and political reforms to open China to the rest of the world. Foreigners started to trickle into China again over the next few years, first through curiosity, then later to set up businesses in China's rapidly expanding economy.

By the time I arrived in Shanghai, Chinese students had already begun to gain access to information from the outside world for the first time through books and other media that were brought into the country by foreigners. My Chinese friends were hungry for anything I could tell them about the outside world, as at that stage it was still impossible for many of them to leave China to see for themselves.

As communism began to collapse in Europe, the youth of China became restless, demanding more freedom and a chance to have a say in the way their country was ruled. Students and activists began to stage peaceful protests in public places throughout China, particularly in major cities. China was undergoing rapid reforms and young people truly believed that things could change, that they would be listened to, that they could make a difference. They wanted to be heard.

— Sally Rippin

1

The lights turned green at the intersection of Huai Hai and Hua Shan roads and a hundred or more cyclists lunged forward dinging their bells. An old lady hopped back onto the footpath to avoid the crush.

From a stop up ahead, a battered white bus lurched into the street. A young cyclist broke from the mass, squinting into the pollution and pedaling fast. The bus steadied and groaned and the cyclist pedaled faster, faster, until he was in line with its rear window. Leaning toward the bus, he drew close and stretched out his hand, arching his fingers. Just as the bus ground up a gear and seemed to churn out of reach, the young man grabbed hold of the open window.

Chenxi perched both feet on the rusted bar of his Flying Pigeon bicycle and was carried through the steamy streets of Shanghai, his thick black ponytail flipping in the wind.

At the corner of Yandang Lu, where the music from the conservatory drifted through the dappled light of the plane trees, the bus slowed to turn left. Chenxi waited until the last minute then pushed off. Feet still up on the bar, he rolled halfway down the cul-de-sac before the bike wobbled to a halt. He chuckled. Next time if he pushed off a little harder he might make it right to the end of the street.

Chenxi lowered a foot to the pavement. He dug into the pocket of his baggy army surplus trousers and pulled out a folded piece of paper, smoothing it flat with his ink-stained fingers. He needn't have bothered looking at it. In this quiet street there was only one building where a foreigner would live. He squinted up at the shining tower that overlooked Fuxing Park. Black gates, freshly painted, discouraged any local visitors. A sentry lounged in the gateway sipping green tea from a Nescafé jar.

In 1989, foreigners in China lived differently from the locals. It was not only their obvious wealth, but the way that they never completely integrated: driving around in their shiny cars like goldfish in glass bowls and living high above street level. Chenxi was curious to find out what lay behind all that double-glazing.

He pushed back the sweaty bangs from his forehead. Just the day before a German student had said that, with his long ponytail and baggy khaki trousers, he could almost pass for a foreigner. Overseas Chinese perhaps, or even Japanese? He wheeled his bike forward. He would see just how Japanese he could look.

"Eh!" the sentry called out, suddenly alert.

Chenxi ignored him and put his hand on the gate.

"Ay! Ay! Ay! Ay!" The old man stood up. "*Gan ma?*"

Chenxi pushed the gate open.

"*Tamade!*" The old man swore to himself in Shanghainese. He strode toward Chenxi. "What do you think you are doing, boy?"

Chenxi sniggered before turning around. The old dog had switched from dialect to Mandarin. He had fallen for Chenxi's bluff. These old guys never used Mandarin to speak to locals. Maybe he really could pass for a foreigner? He decided to see how far he could go with his pretense. Smiling a polite smile, he said, in his most scholarly Mandarin, "I live here!"

"Rubbish!" the old man snarled, reverting to Shanghainese. "I know everyone who lives here! Who are you? What do you want?"

Chenxi rolled his eyes theatrically. "I'm visiting someone!"

The old sentry sneered. He had only one responsibility in life. It wasn't a big one, but he would use his meager power for all it was worth.

"Listen," he hissed, making sure Chenxi heard each word. "Under no circumstance whatsoever will I allow you to enter this building. Not today, not tomorrow, not ever! Now, get lost!"

Chenxi shook his head in contempt and pulled the letter out of his pocket. Even before it was unfolded, the official red stamp shone through the thin rice paper. The old man snatched the letter and held it up, peering at the elaborate calligraphy.

"Shanghai College of Fine Arts," he read aloud after a full minute of silent examination. "Huh! I should have expected it—an art student," he snorted.

Grudgingly, he pushed open the gate. Chenxi wheeled his bike past, extracting the paper from the sentry's trembling hands.

"Next time, you won't be coming in, my son! I'll see to that!" he called after Chenxi. "I'll remember you!"

"Get fucked!" Chenxi said under his breath in English.

"YOU MUST BE CHENKSY," Mr. White said, holding out his hand. Even after three years in Shanghai, where he had set up his engineering company, the pronunciation of Chinese names still escaped him.

"Chen-see," Chenxi corrected and stepped into the room. He made no show of hiding his curiosity at seeing the inside of a foreigner's apartment for the first time.

"Yes, yes, well...sit down, sit down," Mr. White said, gesturing toward the living room. "My daughter, Anna, will be out in a minute."

Chenxi took his time. Wandering down the hallway after Mr. White, he paused to pick up antique vases and peer at Chinese paintings along the way. At an immaculately restored rosewood cabinet he stopped and let his fingers brush over the inlaid mother-of-pearl. "How much you pay for that?"

Mr. White was taken aback. "Er...Three thousand yuan, I think." When he saw the scorn in the young man's face, he added, "I know, I know, I paid too much!" He sat down on one of the ivory silk couches, encouraging Chenxi to do the same.

Instead, Chenxi strolled over to a blue-and-white vase on the

6

windowsill and held it to his ear. He tapped the fine ceramic with his finger and shut his eyes, listening to the resonance. Mr. White winced.

When Anna walked into the room, her father was perched on the edge of the couch, face tense. She looked for the source of his anxiety but something in her had already registered the young man's presence.

Her father cleared his throat. "Chen-see. My daughter…" and the young man turned to face her.

Anna stood transfixed.

"Ming," Chenxi said.

"Excuse me?" said Mr. White and Anna together.

"Ming. Ming dynasty," Chenxi said impatiently.

"Well, yes. Yes, I suppose it is…" Mr. White stammered.

"How much you pay?"

"What? Oh, I don't know. I can't remember. I bought it at the antique market. Look," he said, flustered. "We'd better talk about what Anna needs for her art classes. She has a bike, I've arranged that, although I expect for the first week or so she might want to go by taxi. I know you're eighteen, love, but Shanghai is quite tricky to get around. Chen-see, I thought you could take her today to get some brushes, paper, whatever she needs. Here," he said, thrusting a wad of foreign exchange certificates into Chenxi's hand. He guessed the boy had never held FEC before. "That should cover it."

Chenxi flipped through the crisp paper notes, then looked up, grinning. "We can buy whole shop with this!"

Mr. White was used to the bluntness of the locals, but this

one was breathtaking. "That will cover a taxi, too, if you need one, and, er…any other costs you might…" He was about to say "incur," but thought better of it, sorting through his vocabulary carefully for a phrase a Chinese man might understand. "A bit of money for you, too, hey? For your trouble?" He took Chenxi's hand in both of his and patted it.

Anna tried to read Chenxi's eyes. Her father had assured her he knew how to deal with the locals but his obvious condescension toward the young man made her skin prickle. She prided herself on her ability to read faces, but looking at Chenxi Anna was stumped.

"Well, I must get back to work," Mr. White said. "I'll leave you to it. I trust you'll look after Anna, won't you, Chensee? Good, good. Well then, I'm off. My car will be waiting downstairs."

He picked up his black leather briefcase and walked to the door. As his fingers touched the handle, he hesitated and turned. "*Zaijain!*" he said, testing his Chinese. "Goodbye!" He would show the young man that there was no fooling him.

Chenxi nodded, and turned back to the vase he had been studying.

Anna watched the young man as he walked around the room. His movements were assured and graceful. The skin on his sinewy forearms was dark honey and hairless, as if carved from smooth rosewood.

Chenxi turned and found her staring at him. She blushed.

"Would you like some tea?"

"Where is your toilet?"

They had spoken at the same time.

"Sorry? Oh, yes. Over there. That door on the left."

As Chenxi left the room Anna prayed that she had flushed properly, but she needn't have worried. He had only gone to see if it was true that foreigners were so rich they sat on toilet seats of gold. Chenxi was out again immediately, smiling to himself at the money he would make from his classroom bet.

"**F**or paint traditional Chinese style," Chenxi announced, "you must learn how master Four Treasures. Number one treasure is brush."

Anna picked up the light bamboo brush and turned it over in her hand. It was smooth and speckled brown like a bird's egg and the long white bristles were hardened to a fine point. She signed her name in a spiral of air-calligraphy before putting it back in the embroidered silk box. She looked up at Chenxi.

He frowned at the brushes nestled in their frivolously decorative box. "Too expensive!"

Anna sighed and placed them back on the dusty display shelf.

Chenxi called to the skinny young man who was picking at his teeth as he leaned against the counter. The man yawned and slid open a metal drawer behind him. Taking out a handful of identical brushes he tossed them on the counter in front of

Chenxi before taking up his original position and resuming work on his teeth.

Chenxi held the brushes one by one and inspected them. First he closed his eyes and jiggled the weight of the brush in his palm. Then he took off the long plastic cover and pulled at the bristles. The bristles of one of the brushes came out in a clump in his palm. He snorted and pushed the scraggly brush toward the salesman, who refused to be distracted from his teeth. Chenxi held each of the brushes to one eye and peered down the length before rolling it under his flattened palm on the counter. Each brush received this scrutiny until, of the half dozen, only one remained.

Anna watched, fascinated, as Chenxi commanded another handful of bigger brushes from the bored salesman and went through the same procedure. Then again and again, until ten minutes later she had six perfect brushes of various sizes lying neatly as a pan flute.

"Number two treasure is paper," Chenxi said.

The salesman slid off his stool and shuffled over to the wide shelves of stacked and folded rice paper. He pushed his glasses up onto his forehead and massaged the bridge of his nose as he stood waiting for Chenxi's order. Choosing the second treasure seemed an easier task. Chenxi gave instructions to the salesman, who heaved a roll of paper off the shelf and brought it to the counter.

"For start student *xuan zhi* is OK," Chenxi said.

He picked up a corner of the paper and pressed his tongue against it. When he pulled it away the damp paper was transparent. Chenxi nodded and helped the salesman peel off five long sheets.

"Third and fourth treasure: ink stone and ink stick."

Anna raised her eyebrows. Chenxi rummaged through a worn cardboard box on the counter. He chose a cellophane-wrapped ink stick and passed it to Anna. She looked at the long black block of ink in her palm. It wasn't as intricately decorated as some of those on display—Chenxi was economizing—but with its twisted gold and red dragons, silver-embossed clouds and etched calligraphy, it still looked too pretty to use. While Anna was wondering how ink was made from this solid block, Chenxi crossed the room.

On another counter a surly woman had placed four identical ink stones, all of them smooth and as dark as coal dust. On each was a flat circular stone lid, which Chenxi tested for an exact fit. He held his ear to the hollow scraping noise as he twisted the lids and rejected all four of them. The woman let out an exasperated grunt and rummaged under the counter.

"Oh, that one looks fine to me!" Anna protested, trying to please, but Chenxi glared at her.

As if to prove Anna's ignorance, Chenxi rejected the next three stones, and the saleswoman searched under the counter again. Groaning, she laid out in turn the last five she had in stock, and stood back, arms crossed, lips pressed. Anna tried to exchange a sympathetic smile with her, but the woman looked away.

The last stone passed the test and Chenxi carried the fourth treasure to yet another counter where the first three had been wrapped in bundles of brown paper and string. Chenxi pulled out a clump of grubby notes from his pocket, counting them to another saleswoman sitting in a booth. That's odd, Anna thought, didn't my father give him new banknotes?

The woman checked the money. After writing in a large receipt book, she tore off yellow, white, and pink pages and used a large bulldog clip to attach them to the notes. She fastened this to a pulley and string, which began in the booth at desk height and stretched right across the shop.

Anna watched the money and the receipts jiggle up along the string, over her head, until they disappeared into a small hole near the ceiling on the other side of the room. A few minutes later, the bundle jiggled back down, minus the notes and the pink sheet of paper, but with the addition of a small plastic coin bag.

The saleswoman unclipped the two remaining sheets of paper, now adorned with a sticky red stamp, and handed the white copy to Chenxi. The yellow copy she put into a drawer, then tossed a few plastic coins from the small bag across the counter to him. He pocketed the coins and handed the receipt to Anna, who was struggling with all the brown paper packages, and then sauntered out of the shop.

In the street after the cool darkness of the art shop, Anna wondered how much time had passed. She had only been in Shanghai a day and it was easy to lose track of where she was amid the damp gray heat, the unfamiliar smells of fish and rancid bean curd, and the constant ebb and flow of the crowds. It was the beginning of April, but the heat was so different from the cool spring days she was familiar with in San Francisco. She hoped she would get used to the heat soon as she only had four weeks in Shanghai to study at the art college and, now that she had met Chenxi, Anna knew they would go quickly.

Chenxi hailed a taxi. As they slipped into the air-conditioning, Anna felt light-headed. Was it the heat outside or the proximity of Chenxi's smooth arm to her mottled pink one?

From the backseat it was impossible to see through the crowds of bicycles. The driver, one hand on the wheel, one on the horn, inched forward, the sea of cyclists opening to let him pass, then closing behind him. Occasionally Anna felt a bicycle bump off the car body. The smiling face of Mao swung in a red-tasseled frame from the rearview mirror. "Why would he have a photo of a dead leader in his taxi?" Anna laughed.

"To protect him," Chenxi said. "Some years ago, two taxi drivers have a bad accident and only one driver not killed. He have portrait of Mao in his taxi and he tell everyone that is why he not die in this terrible accident. Now many taxi drivers have Mao in their taxis. To keep them safe. Old China very superstitious country."

He winked at Anna and her heart skipped a beat. Feeling her cheeks flush under Chenxi's gaze, she turned back to look out the window on her side. From the radio came the whining and cymbal clashing of Beijing opera. A large Nescafé jar of what looked like warm pondweed sloshed between the driver's thighs. Now and then he picked it up and opened the lid expertly with one hand, slurping from its contents.

Chenxi chatted with the driver, who glanced into the mirror

to get a better look at Anna. He seemed captivated by her blond unruly hair, which frizzed disobediently in the humid Shanghai weather. She sat with the parcels on her lap and stared out the window. Her cooling sweat, along with the fine down on Chenxi's arm, pricked her skin into goosebumps. She wished she could think of something to say to him, but felt girlish and shy. Now was the opportunity, she scolded herself, running through her repertoire of opening lines.

At a red traffic light, just as Anna had the phrase she was searching for, Chenxi sat upright. He wound down his window and shouted at someone. Anna strained to see who he was calling, but a hundred identical faces stared in at her.

Chenxi turned to her, smiling. "He my school friend. You OK I leave you go home? Him driver know where you home. I go with my friend?"

He touched Anna on the knee.

"Of course…" And he was gone, whistling and yelping into the crowd. A light fingerprint tingled the skin on her knee. She looked up and the driver's narrow eyes stared at her. Anna turned back to the window.

The crowded street emptied into a lane where children scattered, and washing hung from bamboo poles overhead. In darkened doorways, walnut-faced old ladies squatted over plucked feathers and vegetable peelings. Anna knew at once that this wasn't the way she had come with Chenxi. She bit the inside of her cheek.

The driver slowed to a halt.

Anna leaned forward, alarmed. "Yandang Apartments!"

she cried, waving the scrap of paper her father had given her.
"Yandang Lu!"

"OK, OK, OK!" The driver shooed away her hand. He opened his door and sidled out of the cab, which steamed and ticked in the heat. Instantly, snub noses pressed against the windows. Everyone had come to inspect her. The roar of the traffic sounded far away. Anna sat back, her heart flipping like a fish, and stared ahead. On the radio, the opera was building in tempo—cats wailing and saucepans crashing. Chairman Mao beamed malevolently down at her.

The driver returned with an old woman on one arm and a huge watermelon in the other. Around him, his family stared in at the pale sweating foreigner and called, "Hellooo! Hellooo!" The old woman, with staring yellow eyes and a gummy smile, reached in from the driver's open door and touched Anna's head, nodding and cooing as her fingers fondled Anna's hair.

Finally, when his family had all enjoyed a look, the driver got back in the taxi, set the watermelon on the seat beside him, and started the engine. From the lane, the car eased back into familiar traffic. Anna's face burned in anger and humiliation at having been treated like a circus freak by the taxi driver, and because Chenxi had deserted her. She swore she would never allow herself to be so easily taken advantage of again. Chenxi was being paid good money to look after her! Next time she wouldn't allow herself to fall for his charms.

3

Day dissolved into evening. The colors of the sunset tinged the smoggy gray sky. Restaurants opened. Men in suits with fake designer labels sewn on the cuffs squatted in the doorways, smoking. A noodle seller packed up his stall to make way for the competition. The people who ate this late wouldn't be interested in a bowl of noodles. Night dining was for foreigners, for making deals, for exchanging cigarettes and handshakes. Spending money to make money. All beyond this old man. He earned enough to get by with his noodle soup and ration tickets. Making money was for young people. For them it was about getting rich to go to America. He considered himself fortunate just to have survived the terrors of the past.

He swept the concrete pavement in front of his stall. Noodles, spit, and cockroaches swirled into the gutter. Night fell and a breeze lifted the damp heat of the day. The old man wiped his hand across his smeary brow. "Come on, you two," he said to the youths in the back corner. "I want to go home."

The two young men looked up from their conversation, surprised to find that darkness had crept in around them. Chenxi dragged on the butt of his cigarette, the orange glow lighting his face, then flicked it out into the street. "Sorry, Gramps. We're going, we're going."

His friend, Lao Li, unwound his gangling legs from beneath the grimy Formica table and stood up, ducking to miss the swinging lightbulb as he headed for the door.

"Here, Gramps," Chenxi said, draping his arm around the old man's shoulder. He winked and slipped a note into the withered hand. "For your trip to America!"

The two young men guffawed as they vaulted onto the rusty bikes that leaned against the stall.

The old man looked into his palm at the brand new FEC shining there. He watched the youths wheel off down the deserted street and shook his head. What trouble were they up to now?

"HEY, LET'S GO TO A BAR!" Chenxi said, his cheeks flushed and his spirit daring from the rice wine he had shared with his friend. He rode ahead and looped a figure eight until Lao Li caught up. "What do you say? The fancy one on Huai Hai Lu?"

Lao Li grinned, his speech slurred. "You can't go there! It's for foreigners!"

Chenxi patted the wad of FEC in his pocket. "I'm Japanese

and you're from Taiwan!"

Lao Li laughed. "They'll never believe us!"

"Come on, man. Money talks. Foreign money talks the loudest of all!"

Lao Li shook his head. But he knew he would follow his crazy friend. He always did.

SNICKERING AND SNORTING, Chenxi and Lao Li hid their bikes in the shrubbery near the entrance to the bar. Chenxi did his shirt up to the neck to hide his tattered undershirt and Lao Li slicked back the floppy strands of his bangs. They looked at each other, pulling serious faces before bursting into laughter again.

A heavily made-up local girl with a short skirt and high heels tripped by, hanging on the arm of a well-dressed foreigner. She glanced at Chenxi's handsome face as she passed. The foreign man held open the heavy glass door for her and they slipped into the smoke and sultry music.

"OK," whispered Chenxi. "Let's go."

A stone-faced Chinese man in a dinner suit stood at the door with his arms crossed. As Chenxi and Lao Li approached, the man frowned and his head sank back into his neck.

"Hi!" Chenxi said in English. "We here meet some friends."

The doorman continued to stare into the bushes.

Chenxi tried another tactic. Slipping into Mandarin, he pleaded, "Come on, man, my friend's hurt. We've got to get him inside. He needs something to drink!"

Lao Li grabbed his throat on cue, gasping and nodding.

No response.

"Here," Chenxi said, resorting to Shanghainese. "A little something for your trouble." He pulled out the wad of FEC and fanned himself with it. The man stared straight ahead. Chenxi picked out one of the notes and slipped it into the man's top pocket, the way he had seen them do in American movies. The man didn't blink. Chenxi reached for the door. Out slid the doorman's fat hand to trap Chenxi's wrist in a firm grip. This time he looked straight into Chenxi's eyes. They stood locked like that for many heartbeats, until Lao Li put his hand on his friend's shoulder.

"Come on, Chenxi. Let's go."

"No way!" Chenxi muttered, still staring into the unblinking face. "I'm going in."

The heavy glass door swung open. A small Chinese man with a hairy mole on his cheek stepped out of the smoke and the music. He finished his conversation with someone inside before turning and smiling at Chenxi.

"Now, what seems to be the problem?" he said to Chenxi in Shanghainese.

Chenxi tried to remember who had said he looked Japanese. He wasn't fooling anyone.

"No problem," Chenxi smiled back. "Just want to go in for a drink."

"You know that's not possible," the manager said, shaking a long fingernail at Chenxi. Two big Chinese men appeared on either side of him. Both of them were dressed in stylish gray suits and glared ominously.

"Come on, Chenxi," Lao Li whispered.

"I have FEC," Chenxi said. He emphasized the acronym as if it was the secret code to his entry. The code that would open all doors.

"That's nice," said the man pleasantly. "You can spend it in America then!" And he turned toward the door.

Chenxi stepped forward. The two big men in suits stepped in front of him, blocking the entrance to the bar. One of them sneered, daring him to attempt to push past them. Chenxi raised his hand—a feeble gesture of peace—but a fist seemed to shoot out from nowhere, catching him on the shoulder. He found himself reeling. A slow second passed. His skull hit the pavement with a thud.

The manager shook his head and turned back to the entrance, his men closing in behind him. Chenxi lay still, waiting for his vision to come back into focus, waiting for the anger rising in him to subside. Lao Li crouched beside him. Chenxi sat up and dabbed the back of his head with his fingertips, feeling the sticky blood. The doorman stared down at him.

"Come on," Lao Li urged. "Let's get out of here!"

For an instant Chenxi thought of charging. It would mean he would shed more blood, and it would almost be worth it to mess up their crisp white shirts. But Lao Li was at his side, imploring Chenxi to walk away.

Chenxi stood up and spat. "I wouldn't want to drink your fuckin' foreign wine, anyway."

Anna woke to the sound of music. Loud and crackly, sentimental jazz. And behind that, a high-pitched counting in Chinese numbers, keeping time. Anna knew that beat. One, two, three...Two, two, three. A waltz?

In a daze, she sat up. Her surroundings, the new noises, they all drew together in her mind like pieces of a puzzle. Her father let out a snore in the next room. The puzzle snapped into place. Her second day in Shanghai was about to start.

Kicking the cotton sheet from her sweaty body, Anna shuffled along the bed to where she could sit by the window. From the thirteenth floor, she had a clear view of Fuxing Park. Directly beneath her was a group of waltzers. There were about twenty of them, mostly women dancing with other women, while an instructor on the side kept time through a megaphone. Anna giggled. Waltzing at six o'clock in the morning! She would have to write all this down before it seemed commonplace to her.

From her bedside drawer, Anna pulled out the journal her mother had given her a few days before she left San Francisco. Perhaps her mother had instinctively known that she wouldn't be hearing from her daughter much, once Anna arrived in Shanghai, and the journal was a way of staying close. Anna was relieved to have some time away from her mother, who had become too dependent on her. Now that her mother didn't have a husband to lean on, Anna felt like she had been forced to become her emotional support and confidante. Let one of my sisters deal with her moods for a change, Anna thought. I'm here for a break. For an adventure!

She smoothed open the first page of the small book.

April 4th, 1989

Here I am, finally, in Shanghai! I'm looking out of my bedroom window from Dad's apartment and the view is amazing. I can see right over Fuxing Park. It's only six a.m. but already the park is full of life—it's like my own private entertainment! Below me there are waltzers and, to the right of them, a solitary old man hugs a tree. Behind him, another old man jiggles on the spot. Across a path lined with peonies, tai-chi is beginning. I watch the slow perfect fanning of limbs.

I could sit at this window for hours, days, weeks; the park is like an ever-changing Bruegel painting with minute detail to be discovered. But unfortunately I don't have months in Shanghai, only weeks, and even though I thought my time here with Dad would drag, I'm not so sure now. I've only been here a day but I already have a date (sort of) with the most beautiful-looking

23

man I have ever laid eyes on! So I have to get moving, because he's picking me up in just over an hour.

What to wear? I wish it wasn't so hot because I've brought all the wrong clothes and I can't imagine how I'll find anything here to fit me. All the girls in Shanghai are so tiny. I feel like a great hulking sweaty blob! And they all seem to wear frilly girly dresses and high heels—very different from my shorts and jeans. I wonder if Chenxi likes girls in jeans?

Anna's father's alarm rang through the thin plaster wall and she crept out of bed to use the shower before he did. Then she slipped on a pair of shorts and a t-shirt, the lightest clothing she had brought with her, and joined her father in the kitchen.

They ate breakfast together. Muesli and milk, toast and jam. If you had FEC you could shop at the foreign supermarkets and eat the same food as back home.

Before he left for work, Mr. White slipped a few more of the banknotes into Anna's hand. They seemed to grow inside his wallet. Then he added some advice on how to get by in Shanghai. "Remember, *xie xie* is thank you, and don't eat at the street stalls. The Hilton Hotel has a good hamburger restaurant if you need lunch."

"It's OK, Dad. I'll be with Chenxi. He's coming to pick me up for college today." She had decided it would be better not to mention yesterday's desertion if she wanted her father to continue paying Chenxi to be her translator and guide.

"Yes, look darling, I know it sounds like fun to study a bit of Chinese painting, but don't feel you have to go. I've got plenty of good videos here and you can catch a taxi into town to meet me for lunch, if you like. You're on holidays, remember? I'll take you to the consulate on Friday night for drinks. You might meet some foreign students your age that you can make friends with."

"Chenxi is my age, Dad. He's only nineteen," Anna reminded her father.

Mr. White stood in front of the hallway mirror to adjust his tie, ignoring her response. "Hey, they've got a pool at the consulate! You could go for a swim today. That would be fun, wouldn't it? It's very hot to be riding all the way out to the college."

Anna was irritated by her father's protectiveness. And why did he have to assume that she would want to share his sheltered expatriate lifestyle? She wasn't in China to meet Americans! "I'll see how it goes, Dad. It's not that far. Chenxi took me past the college yesterday on the way to buy my art supplies."

Her father still wasn't listening. He'd had another thought. "I know! Rather than go to the college every day we could get one of the teachers to come out here to teach you. At the apartment. And get that boy, Chenksy, too, to translate."

"Dad! I said I'll see how it goes. I'll be fine, OK?"

"Yes, see how it goes, dear. Just remember to take my work number with you, and plenty of money in case you have any problems." He wiped his mouth on his handkerchief. "And don't worry about cleaning up, the *aiyi* will do it."

AFTER HE LEFT, Anna wandered to the sitting room window that looked over the front door of their building. From here she could see anyone who entered the building or left it. She watched her father get into the back of his navy car with tinted windows and thought how absurd it was that he complained of putting on weight. If he rode to work like the other sixteen million inhabitants of Shanghai, he would be as skinny as they were. Instead, he preferred to pay a fortune to ride a stationary bike in an exclusive "foreigners only" gym.

Seven-thirty came and went, then eight o'clock, then nine. Anna had never been a patient person. She liked looking forward to something, but she hated waiting. By nine-thirty she knew Chenxi wasn't coming. Classes had started over an hour ago and, with a forty-minute bike ride ahead of her, Anna wondered if she would make it to any of the first lessons at all.

Why wouldn't he come? They had spent a great afternoon together the day before—at least she thought so—seeing the sights of Shanghai in the air-conditioned comfort of a taxi. She'd felt giddy sitting so close to him in the backseat, absorbing the smell of him, studying his beautiful face. She'd gone to bed that night dreaming of him, feeling sure he would have done the same about her. If you were attracted to someone, weren't they necessarily attracted to you? But Chenxi's face gave away nothing. The picture of that warm apologetic smile in the taxi before he disappeared into the traffic materialized repeatedly in Anna's mind.

She wasn't sure why she was so obsessed with him. After all, she barely knew him. But there was something about Chenxi that pushed all reason out of her mind. He was so mysterious, so unselfconsciously handsome. She had never felt like this about anyone before. Perhaps he had a girlfriend? Was that why he wasn't coming? If so, he should have made it clear from the start. Surely he could feel Anna's attraction toward him? So why did he smile at her that way? She started to feel angry again.

Wasn't it an honor for him to be chosen out of all the students at the college to look after her? Her father said that any other Chinese student would have cut off his right arm for the opportunity. And all that FEC he'd given Chenxi? According to her father it was virtually impossible for a student in China to get hold of the foreigners' currency—other than by illegal means. Local Chinese currency was supposed to have the same value as the FEC, but it couldn't be exchanged outside China. So one yuan in FEC could be traded for up to twice as many local yuan on the black market. Not only that, but with FEC a Chinese person could buy foreign goods and have access to places where only foreigners were allowed. Chenxi should be grateful for the opportunity they were offering him! Anna stood up, frustrated and irritable. Should she go to the consulate pool after all?

She was deciding whether to exchange the bamboo and wolf-hair paintbrushes in her bag for her bikini when the doorbell rang. Of course he had come, why wouldn't he? She flung the bag over her back and skipped to the door, but a key fiddled in the lock and it was opened before she had a chance to reach it. Both women found themselves face to face with a stranger.

The *aiyi* was the first to speak, "Oh, sorry, sorry. Daughter? You Mr. White daughter?"

"Yes," Anna said, disappointed. "You must be the *aiyi*?"

The young woman looked very dressed up for a cleaning maid. Her hair was tied up at the back in a glittery, gauzy clasp and frizzed out at the front. She wore make-up, a shiny pink blouse and the strappy high heels that seemed to be so fashionable among the women in Shanghai.

"Yes, yes. *Aiyi!*" The Chinese woman giggled at Anna's pronunciation. "Wang. My name Wang. Miss Wang."

"Anna."

Miss Wang beamed. As if in a trance she walked up to Anna and fingered her long blond ringlets, cooing and nodding in approval. Anna stood still to allow the *aiyi* to sate her curiosity, even though she didn't feel comfortable being poked and prodded. Miss Wang stood back to inspect Anna from a distance. "Mmm…*hen piaoliang!*"

Anna shrugged.

The *aiyi* giggled again, then rushed to Mr. White's bookshelf and pulled out a Chinese-English dictionary. She licked her thumb and flicked through the pages. When she found what she wanted, she grinned and brought the book over to Anna, pointing at the word with her finger.

"Pretty," Anna said.

The *aiyi* raised her eyebrows.

"Pre-tty," Anna repeated, more slowly.

"Plitty!" the *aiyi* tried, and Anna smiled encouragingly.

In return she tried out one of the Chinese words she already

28

knew. "*Xie xie!*"

"Sank you?" Miss Wang twittered.

"Yes!" Anna smiled, and then had an idea. "Here," she said, taking the book. She flicked through until she saw the word she was looking for.

"Oh, yes, yes. Taxi!" the *aiyi* said, pleased to have known the word already.

Anna fished her map of Shanghai out of her bag. She found the college in the top left corner and pointed to it. "Can you get me a taxi to go there? Shanghai College of Fine Arts?"

"Oh!" The *aiyi* nodded, squinting at the map. "*Shanghai Mei Shu Xue Yuan!* Oh! Taxi?"

"Yes!" said Anna, excited with their communication. "Yes! Taxi to go there!"

Ten minutes later, Anna was on her way to the college, grinning with pride in her own determination.

Chenxi was at the bar. Everything was blurred and too bright. The man in the smart suit was jabbing him in the shoulder, harder and harder, pushing and shoving.

The jabbing became more urgent. Lao Li's voice murmured a warning in Chenxi's ear. The pitch rose and rose until it was no longer Lao Li's mellow voice, but the screeching of Mrs. Zhu who lived in the apartment next door to Chenxi.

"Get up! Get up, you good for nothing. You're in trouble again. The college has rung for you. Three times. Finally I had to go downstairs and speak to them. If they knew you were slumbering away up here like an old ox. If your mother knew! Out working all day to bring up a great big boy like you. You call yourself an artist? You're a lazy good for nothing..."

"OK, OK, OK," Chenxi groaned. He tried to sit up, but a blinding light burst behind his eyes and he fell back on the pillow again. He rubbed the crusty swelling on his scalp and wondered if the ache in his head was from the rice wine or the fall.

"It's all right, Mrs. Zhu, I'll ring the college. You can go now. Thanks for taking the message." Chenxi flashed a smile and his gruff neighbor was momentarily calmed by the young man's beautiful face.

Yet Mrs. Zhu continued to hover, suspicious. She had looked after her neighbor's son since he was a child, while his mother tried to make a living, picking up factory work where she could. The poor woman, thought Mrs. Zhu. She was lucky she could get any work after all the problems her husband had caused.

Mrs. Zhu liked to keep an eye out for them. And for all the other people in the building. She prided herself on having the most up-to-date information on the private life of every single person in Apartment Block Eighteen. It was her responsibility, she thought, not only as a good tenant, but as a good member of the district Communist Party.

"It's OK, Mrs. Zhu!" Chenxi insisted, dragging himself out of bed. "I'm going to ring them straight away."

The old lady backed out of the doorway, looking around the shuttered room in the dim light for anything out of the ordinary. She shook her head in exasperation and pulled the door closed behind her.

Chenxi stumbled to the window in his underwear and yanked open the blinds. The tiny, dusty room he shared with his mother was illuminated by the late morning sun. Along one wall lay his bed, along another, his mother's. The third wall was filled by a huge cabinet, which served as bookshelf, clothes cupboard, crockery cabinet and television shelf. Everything Chenxi and his mother owned had its place in or on this cabinet, and what was left over fitted ingeniously into crevices between and under beds, behind the door and under stools.

The center of the room was dominated by an ornately carved mah-jong table covered with a thick sheet of glass under which were compressed certificates, birthday cards and photos: an identity photo of Chenxi's mother, a photo of Chenxi as a baby. But the photo of Chenxi's father stayed locked in a drawer.

Chenxi dressed quickly and bounded down the dingy stairwell of Apartment Block Eighteen to the phone booth outside.

"Hello, Uncle," Chenxi said with a grin. He bowed to the old man with the megaphone, whose job it was to shout out phone calls for the residents of the building. It was no use getting on this old man's bad side; Chenxi needed to use the phone too often! The old man nodded back and sipped from his jar of tea. Chenxi perched himself on the edge of the desk and dialed the college.

"MR. DIRECTOR VERY SORRY," translated the young secretary for Anna.

The three of them sat in a triangle around the college director's desk: Anna, the director, and his secretary, who spoke a little English. The director had Chenxi on the other end of the phone.

32

"Mr. Director sorry for many inconveniencing you. Chenxi very bad. He will have lots of trouble. You father very angry, eh?" She seemed particularly anxious about this possibility.

"No, not really," Anna said. "It's not that much trouble. And don't worry, my father doesn't know anything."

She tried to make them feel better, but the atmosphere in the small office was stifling. The director spoke into the receiver in a low terse voice, looking up every now and then, smiling at her. Anna shifted awkwardly. Her thighs stuck to the plastic chair in the heat.

The secretary repeated to herself, "Ah, yes! Chenxi lots of trouble."

Chewing her lip, Anna thought back to her unceremonious arrival. The taxi driver had insisted on bringing Anna right into the college grounds. No sooner had the gatekeeper spied them than he was on the phone to the director, who appeared with his secretary, both horrified to see the foreigner arriving on her own. Anna had been whisked into his office, hundreds of eyes staring down at her from the surrounding windows.

WITHIN MINUTES, Chenxi arrived at the director's office, breathless and sweating, but with the same cool smile on his face.

"Sorry," Anna whispered. What sort of trouble had she caused for him? But Chenxi would not look at her.

The director hissed a few words at Chenxi, then the secretary said, "Chenxi look after you now," and led them out of the office.

They strode down the hall and up two flights of stairs. All along the corridor, boys gawked from the doorways and girls giggled and twisted their hair. Every student watched Chenxi and the foreigner and every one of them had something to say about it.

They entered a large light-filled classroom on the top floor of the college. The cement floor was spattered with paint and the chalky white walls were pockmarked and grubby with fingerprints. Six large wooden desks were stationed around the outskirts of the room and the four boys sitting at them looked up as Anna entered. She was alarmed to discover that there were no girls in her new class.

Lao Li sniggered at Chenxi and raised his eyebrows at the small procession. The other boys in the room whooped and whistled. The teacher tried to call the class back to attention. For an instant, Anna wished she were floating in the consulate pool.

"I hope you enjoy your stay," said the secretary formally, with a hint of a bow to Anna as she left.

The teacher shuffled over to Anna and spoke in a soft voice, holding out his hand to be shaken. He was short and hunched with enormous buck teeth that stuck out so far they prevented his thick lips from closing. His left hand flapped around his sunken chin as if hoping to hide his teeth.

Anna shrugged, and looked to Chenxi for help.

"This is Teacher Dai. Dai Laoshi," Chenxi said, then he added something quickly in Chinese and the whole class laughed. Even Dai Laoshi couldn't suppress a toothy smirk. Anna felt a trickle of sweat run all the way down her calf. She shook Dai Laoshi's hand. It was like holding a small damp frog.

Chenxi spoke again and the five classmates jumped into action, shoving desks and clearing paper until there was a space for Anna in a corner on her own. Dai Laoshi tapped the desk encouragingly. She walked over and sat on the chair beside it. As the class regained order, she laid out her pristine brushes, her ink stick still wrapped in cellophane, her ink stone and her roll of paper. Once the attention had shifted from her, she looked around the room.

The students were painting on silk, each of them with an open book or a duplicate of a painting beside them, copying every intricate brushstroke onto the delicate fabric. Anna was alarmed at the thought of beginning with such a difficult exercise, but she needn't have worried: apparently the teacher was just as doubtful of her painting skills, and advised via Chenxi that she watch until the afternoon class, when they would have life drawing. To be dismissed so readily was not what Anna had anticipated either, but she had caused enough disruption for one morning, so she sat and watched.

Chenxi was working next to Anna, his face devoid of expression, only glancing up to murmur to a lanky boy with floppy bangs at the desk beside him. The boy would stifle a giggle or roar with laughter. But every now and then his eyes flitted over to Anna. She was clearly the subject of their conversation.

Then Anna looked over at a stocky moon-faced boy with yellow teeth who had laid his silk to one side and was working on a small piece of cardboard. When he felt her eyes on him, he lifted his head and grinned, holding up his work. On the cardboard was a drawing of a voluptuous woman with enormous breasts, wild curly hair and bright blue eyes. Underneath it was written: I LOVE YOU! The boys roared in appreciation and Anna reddened.

The class settled back to work and Anna began to relax. Now and then a student would glance at her and smile. Anna looked over at Chenxi when she could, studying his forearms and fine profile, but he was the only one ignoring her.

Half an hour later, Anna heard shouting and thumping out in the corridor. The hum of voices became louder. The students in Anna's class rinsed their brushes and pushed back from their desks, calling out to each other and to friends in other rooms.

The thumping became louder. Along with the excited voices, the sound was deafening. A siren shrieked and a roar of bodies surged along the corridor and thumped down the stairwells. Thinking it was a fire alarm, Anna stood up.

"Eat! Eat!" Chenxi said to Anna, scraping back his chair.

Anna looked at her watch. It was only half past eleven. Lunch? The other boys in the class had already left, leaping and squealing into the corridor. Anna was alone with Chenxi and his tall friend with the floppy bangs. The boy loped over and stuck out a clammy hand to Anna, pushing his hair out of his eyes with his other hand, and grinning.

"Lao Li," he said.

Anna turned to Chenxi.

"His name. Lao Li."

"Low-lee," Anna tried, and the two boys laughed. But not unkindly. Anna scrutinized Chenxi's perfect face. There was never any malice in his eyes, Anna thought, consoled, but there never seemed to be any affection either.

"You eat with us some lunch?" Chenxi asked. Anna picked up her bag and followed them downstairs.

"Why are there no girls in your class, Chenxi?" she asked.

"Chinese girls prefer to do class for sewing or design," he explained. "Traditional Chinese painting usually for men."

It hadn't occurred to Anna that Chinese painting could be considered a masculine thing to do. At her school, art was considered a feminine occupation, and a slack one at that. Great, thought Anna. I'm not doing well if I'm competing with those prissy Chinese girls for Chenxi's attention. She looked down at her heavy leather sandals and tried to imagine her feet in the dainty plastic heels that the local girls wore. The thought made her giggle.

She wondered if Chenxi found her big western body and boyish clothes unattractive. She had always found it easy to lure boys; in the States they liked her big breasts and round hips and she dressed the way all girls her age did. Perhaps, for Chenxi, she was too different to be attractive? She loved everything unfamiliar about him, but maybe she was too foreign for his taste.

They reached the bottom of the stairs and stepped out into

37

the college grounds. "Where you bike?" Chenxi asked.

"I caught a taxi," she admitted, blushing. She knew he already regarded her as a rich foreigner, and she hated to flaunt her money in front of him. "You were supposed to come and pick me up!" she added defensively. She had planned to be cross with him—twice he had let her down—but she hadn't had a chance in the morning's confusion and she felt cheated.

They walked toward the bike shed. Chenxi wrenched a bike from the rusty tangle. "I have show you the way yesterday," he said.

"Not by bike. That was by taxi. How do you expect me to remember that?"

Lao Li circled his bike ahead, waiting. Chenxi shrugged and slung one leg over his seat, then patted the back of his bike. Anna hesitated before clambering awkwardly onto the metal carry rack behind Chenxi. She wasn't sure whether to try to ride side-saddle like the Chinese girls did, but she thought she'd feel safer with her legs on both sides of the bike, so she opted for a self-conscious straddle.

Chenxi turned to face her. "I take you home today after class, then you know which way. Tomorrow you come by yourself, OK?"

Anna looked at him. "Aren't you being paid to look after me?"

"How old you are?" Chenxi asked.

"Eighteen," replied Anna, pleased that he was showing an interest in her.

"Then you old enough to come to school yourself!" He stepped down hard on the pedal and they wobbled off to catch up with Lao Li.

6

The noodle shop was overflowing. People stood in the street hunched over bowls and slurping, or hanging around waiting for a stool.

A young curly-haired Mongol worked the dough on a trestle table at the entrance of the small restaurant. There were smudges of flour on his wind-cracked cheeks. He slapped, folded, and pulled the dough in strips the length of his arm, again and again, until the strips were as fine as spaghetti. Then he twisted off a length and dropped it into the boiling soup. He only looked up when everyone else did, to stare at the foreigner on the back of a Chinese man's bike.

Chenxi acted as if he didn't notice. He and Lao Li parked their bikes and strolled into the shop. Anna brushed off her shorts and followed.

The old man serving up the steaming bowls of noodles pushed a boy off his stool and beckoned for Anna to come in and sit down. Anna looked at the walls spattered with grease and insects, at the grimy tables and the sodden wood chopsticks in baskets. To her right a man cleared his throat and spat on the floor. Her father would be horrified. She was annoyed that Chenxi would expect her to eat in a place like this, but she didn't want to hear his snide remark if she asked to be taken to the Hilton.

"You want that seat?" Chenxi asked, pointing to the vacant stool.

"Er, no, I'm not hungry, actually," Anna said. "I think I'll walk back to class." Chenxi shrugged and took the seat for himself.

Anna inched out of the shop and set off in the direction they had come from. She had tried to pay attention during the ride, but at times, balancing on the back of Chenxi's bike, her arms around his waist, it had been hard not to shut her eyes and breathe in the pleasure of being close to him. Why couldn't she stay angry with him for any length of time?

As Anna wandered back in what she hoped was the direction of the college she recognized the rancid smell of Suzhou Creek, which ran behind the market street. Chenxi must have skirted it on his way to the noodle shop. She remembered that back in the States her father had spoken to her and her sisters about this infamous river long before he'd seen it himself. This river— where people lived on houseboats, fished, and washed their vegetables—was so polluted that it boiled twice a year because of the methane gases trapped beneath its surface.

Her father had launched the engineering company in Shanghai that had made an attempt to clean the river, but after a three-year delay caused by complicated and unfamiliar bureaucracy, everyone had given up and gone home. Only Anna's father had stubbornly persisted, on the pretext that he refused to leave a job unfinished.

The first time Anna visited her father in Shanghai, two years ago, he took her and her two younger sisters across the river. As the taxi crawled over the bridge, Mr. White lecturing proudly to his uninterested daughters, they had wound up the windows to block out the stink. Anna and her sisters peered down, revolted, at the ooze of rainbow-slicked water where fish floated belly-up and rats scrabbled among the debris on the banks.

Anna's mother always said that taking the job in Shanghai was a convenient escape from the family; returning home would mean he would have to deal with all the problems he had left behind. When the job in China had come up, Anna's mother willingly took on the role of the martyr, and stayed in San Francisco so that the girls' schooling would not be disrupted. Anna knew that her mother, with her sighs and her long afternoons in bed with the blinds closed, was a difficult person to leave, and that if her father had been a more honest man he wouldn't have used the job as an excuse. Anna had found it hard enough to extricate herself from her mother's cloying neediness even to visit her father in Shanghai for four weeks.

She also knew that, while her father put up a very good pretense at being overjoyed to have his eldest daughter staying with him, she was a daily reminder of those family problems, that unfinished business. And there was nothing he claimed to hate more than a job unfinished.

Soon Anna arrived at the entrance of the bustling market. The stench of the creek mingled with the odors of livestock and manure. She passed a weathered farm girl selling persimmons from a frayed mat and offered her a tentative smile. The young woman jumped up, grabbing a handful of the ripe fruit, and trotted behind Anna, jabbering loudly. A set of brass and leather scales was balanced on her forefinger. Anna shook her head but the woman ran back and forth, adding more and more persimmons to the metal bowl. Anna kept shaking her head and smiling. The woman, mistaking this for some complicated bargaining game, gave up with a frustrated shout.

Peasants snoozed on top of cartloads of watermelons and cabbages, or squatted beside woven straw mats where a few damaged tomatoes were displayed. Schoolchildren with red scarves around their necks were chewing on long sticks of sugarcane. When they had sucked the juice dry, they spat out the woody pulp. A young man by a cart scraped off the knobbly purple skin with a huge cleaver and handed more glistening white canes to the children. The juice dribbled down their chins.

Anna felt hot and thirsty, but she didn't have the courage to mime and point in front of the crowd to ask for a piece of sugarcane. Already the children were looking up and nudging each other, calling out, "*Wai guo ren! Wai guo ren!* Foreigner! Foreigner!"

She turned and stumbled through the fish market.

Fish in plastic tubs writhed and thrashed or bobbed limply in the water. A crowd had gathered around a housewife bargaining for a turtle. The turtle's legs were bound with raffia and it hung upside down from a scale-spattered fist. Its pointed head bobbed in and out of the folds of its neck like the tip of a small boy's penis.

As she passed tubs of eels, Anna stared, repulsed but fascinated: the fishmonger took them live and thrashing, pressed their heads onto a nail in a wooden board, then slit them open and peeled their intestines from them.

The road became darker and stickier. Hunks of meat dribbled on stone tables. Carcasses with bones like mother-of-pearl hung from hooks. Old women squatted beneath them, shoveling rice into their mouths from tin bowls and waving flies from the congealed blood.

The heat suddenly became too much for Anna. Her head felt light. She shuffled forward, trying to keep her eyes ahead, but they were drawn magnetically to the festering charcuterie. She was reminded of the time back home with her family, sitting in the back of a hot car in a traffic jam, as they approached the flashing lights of a road accident. She willed her eyes not to turn and gawk, as all the others in the safety of their cars were doing. She told herself she didn't need that perverse voyeurism. But at the last moment, just as her father changed gears to speed past the twisted metal and shattered glass, her eyes flicked to the side as if of their own accord. The whole scene was scorched into her mind, the black, the blue, and the red.

The only thing that kept her from fainting right there in the marketplace was the thought of waking up in all that blood and filth.

WHEN SHE ARRIVED at the college grounds Anna was relieved the students weren't back from lunch. It was now twelve-thirty. She hadn't thought to ask what time the afternoon classes began. Inside the cement building it was cooler. How could it be so hot when there appeared to be no sun? Every day since she arrived had been humid, but the sun never broke through the gray clouds. And it was still only spring! Anna pictured Shanghai from above, simmering away like a pressure cooker under its dome of pollution.

Dragging herself up the echoing stairwell, she prayed that the classroom would be empty so she could rest her head on her desk. She was now feeling ill. Perhaps she would catch a taxi to the apartment and her air-conditioned bedroom. She could even get an earlier flight home. A month was a long time to stay in a strange country, and it wasn't as if she was really going to learn anything at the college. How could she when she spoke no Chinese? She couldn't even make friends. The only person who spoke English was Chenxi and he was clearly not interested in her.

That's what she would do: stay a couple of weeks and then go back to San Francisco and hang out with her friends until university began. She had already deferred the first year of her studies through pure indecision, fooling around in and out of sales jobs until her father suggested she come to stay with him for a while. To have some "serious talks" about her future.

Anna suddenly experienced the sickening feeling of wasting

time. She didn't know which felt more pointless: her ridiculous crush on Chenxi or her fruitless desire to study painting. Either way, her father wouldn't have to persuade her. She would definitely be ready to go to university next year.

Chenxi was pressed up against the wall. He had finished working on one part of the paper and was now on a stool reaching for the top corner. Layer after layer of brushstrokes, building up a gradual blackness. Waves of gray rippling around him, a series of indentations sharpening in contrast.

In the top right corner, drips of ink bled into the porous rice paper, pale gray spatters like the speckles of a hen's egg. Below this area were dark black slashes of dry brushstrokes over wet, pointing upwards and inwards like ragged mountain peaks or perhaps even an exposed ribcage. The corner that Chenxi now painted was a combination of soft gray brushstrokes and dark wet dribbles of black ink—matted hair or foliage, it was impossible to tell.

He never paused to inspect his work. It grew beneath him of its own accord, breathing, taking life under the gentle encouragement of its creator. Each stroke of the brush like the unearthing of an archaeological treasure. There was nothing familiar about his abstract melding of shapes and shades, but it was as harmoniously complete as the work of any Master, from the East or the West.

Chenxi stood back. Lao Li opened his eyes groggily and glanced at him from his chair tilted up against the windowsill. "You finished?"

"There's someone at the door," Chenxi said without taking his eyes off his work.

Lao Li looked over and, sure enough, the foreigner was peering in through the glass. "How did you know?" Lao Li said, getting up to let her in.

"She's been there for a while. I wondered how long it would take her to find her way back."

Lao Li unlocked the classroom door and let Anna in. Chenxi began pulling the pins out of the huge sheet of paper tacked to the wall.

"Wait," said Anna. "Can I look at it?"

Chenxi shrugged and pushed the pins back in.

Anna sat on the end of her desk. She looked at the painting again, without the screen of the dusty glass.

Chenxi leaned against the wall, his arms crossed tight over his chest. "What you think?" he said.

Anna squinted and chewed at the inside of her lip. "I think if you want to give the impression that the foreground is separate from the background you need to darken that circular bit there..."

Chenxi turned in surprise.

"Or otherwise that middle strip needs to be lighter. No, I think darkening that bit would be more effective, don't you?" She looked over at Chenxi. His mouth was gaping. Lao Li was watching them and grinning.

"Er...yes. That what I think before. I do not know if better have darker or lighter..."

"That's only my opinion," Anna added. "Otherwise, I think it's truly beautiful. It's so serene and at the same time full of energy..."

"Serene?"

"Tranquil. Calm. Peaceful."

Chenxi nodded.

"That little rippling bit over there is what brings the whole work together." Anna went to inspect it more closely. It seemed to vibrate in front of her.

Chenxi moved toward her. He cleared his throat. "I not sure about this part. Maybe too much?"

Anna stepped back a little. "No, it's good. You've just been working on it too long. You have to put it away and bring it out again in a few days to look at it with fresh eyes. It's really lovely, Chenxi. When you work out that foreground and background bit, it should be finished. It will be completely harmonious."

"Harmonious?"

"Balanced. Equal. Er...you know, like two opposites that can't exist without the other."

Chenxi smiled. "You mean like yin and yang?"

This time it was Anna's turn to look puzzled.

"Yin and yang. Night and day. Woman and man..."

"That's right!"

Chenxi turned to Anna and for the first time looked her straight in the eye. "Mmm. You give me good compliment," he said, and it seemed an immeasurable time passed before he looked away again.

Anna felt her face burning. She had reached him. She had never expected it to happen this way. Suddenly, when everything had only moments ago felt so wrong, her whole world clicked into place. She held Chenxi's gaze for as long as she dared and imagined herself pulling him into her arms and kissing his honey-smooth face all over. *So this is what they mean about finding your other half in life? I am yin and he is yang.* She knew now that she couldn't ignore her feelings for him. Her fatalist heart told her this was meant to be.

There was a knock at the door and Lao Li lumbered over to answer it.

Chenxi turned back to the wall and pulled the pins out of his work one by one. He rolled the paper up and put it under his desk. Not once did he look at Anna.

The short moon-faced boy entered. Sensing something different in the room, he looked around suspiciously, then walked over to drag an easel from a corner. Lao Li came to attention, jumped up, and did the same. Anna stood, but Lao Li signaled for her to stay put and brought her over an easel. He smiled at her.

"*Xie xie*," she tried.

"*Bu yong xie*," he answered, this time without laughing. "You're welcome."

Lao Li set up Anna's easel with paper, and when he noticed she had no charcoal he fetched her some of his own. Chenxi busied himself with his own easel, but Anna noticed that he glanced over from time to time.

After the other students had arrived and set up their easels, Teacher Dai walked in with a young peasant woman. She was wrapped in a blue and white batik robe and blushed when she saw Anna. She whimpered something to Dai Laoshi, all the while staring at Anna like a frightened animal, but he patted her shoulder, and sat her down in a large cane chair.

"She do not want take clothes off with foreign devil in room!" Chenxi whispered mischievously. "She's from the countryside. She maybe never seen foreign devil before. She think you eat her... how you say?... inside spirit."

Soul, Anna thought to herself, and to Chenxi said, "Tell her I've drawn lots of nude models before."

Chenxi smiled and nodded, but didn't translate. Anna didn't mind. She felt they now shared a secret bond that excluded the rest of the class. The thought of it sparked through her like electricity.

She was touched at how mature the boys were with the model. She looked around and saw they had all begun to draw the peasant woman with her dressing gown on. Obviously if the model wanted to stay fully clothed then there was no debate. So Anna began to draw. She hadn't drawn anything for months now, since the end of school, and it took her a while to warm up, but before long her hand loosened, and once again seemed to move of its own accord.

By Anna's third sheet of paper, the young model had fallen asleep in the thick heat of the classroom. Her head lolled to one side and the top of her gown had fallen open, revealing a small creamy breast. Her long hair fanned across her pale chest, black against white. Anna was shading the ripples of the young woman's ribs when she felt the teacher come up behind her and click his tongue in approval and surprise. She was pleased with how the drawing was coming along.

"Mmm... *Bu zuo! Bu zuo!*" he muttered before moving on.

"He say, 'not bad,'" Chenxi whispered from behind his easel.

"Not bad?" Anna raised her eyebrows, disappointed at the teacher's modest praise.

Chenxi chuckled. "In China, teacher never say very good. He just say, not bad! If your teacher tell you *bu zuo*, you are very happy. Only ninety-year-old Master can be *hen hao*—very good! You like all foreigners. Too proud!"

Anna frowned. She wasn't used to this sort of criticism. Unable to hold back her curiosity, she inched over to see Chenxi's work and was struck to discover how ordinary it was.

"It shit!" Chenxi scoffed.

She had to admit he was right. Especially after what she had witnessed only half an hour earlier. The drawing had no feeling. The proportions were perfect, everything was in the right place, but the woman in the picture could have been anyone. She had no warmth, no distinguishing features, her face was a blank mask, her body that of a statue. Anna was reminded of propaganda posters of happy workers from the USSR in the

1950s. Strong, healthy-looking people, but all identical. Man, woman and child, all done to a formula.

Anna strolled over to where Lao Li was working. Identical. The same picture, just from a different angle. Moon-Face's picture was much the same again. All perfectly produced factory-line drawings. And the teacher walking around behind them, nodding approval or straightening up a few lines here and there.

The studied unity was sinister. This wasn't a coincidence. Was this a forced style, a compromise? Were the students told to paint this way, or did they merely anticipate what was expected of them?

Looking at Chenxi now, his face vacant as he worked on his sketch, she wondered if she really had glimpsed into who he might be.

RIDING HOME IN SILENCE on the back of Chenxi's bike, Anna thought about how she could ask him the questions that crowded her mind. As he dodged through the traffic, she pictured them sitting on the ivory silk couch in her father's quiet apartment. She would make him tea and they would sit and chat. They would get to know each other, maybe kiss.

When they reached the corner of Anna's street, she called out to Chenxi from behind, "You will come in for a drink?"

Chenxi slowed as they approached her gate and pulled up on the opposite side of the road.

Anna slid off the bike, waiting for his reply.

"No, thank you," he said, glancing over at the sentry.

Anna was taken aback. Was he being intentionally contrary? "Come on! You've just ridden all this way. Come upstairs and sit down for a while. You'd be crazy to ride all that way back in this heat. Just come in for a drink?"

Out of the corner of her eye she could see the sentry peering at the pair of them.

"No, thank you. I must go home," Chenxi said, swinging his leg back over his bike. "I see you tomorrow at school."

Bewildered, Anna watched him ride down the street. She watched him until he turned the corner and she couldn't see him anymore.

8

M r. White knew everyone at the Shanghai Hilton. Here he seemed important and respected. The Italian restaurant had reserved his regular table and the manager asked about the special lady accompanying him that night. He winked at Anna, letting her in on the joke, but Anna wondered how many special ladies had sat with her father at his regular table since he had been in China. He wasn't living with her mother anymore, Anna reminded herself; her parents were separated in all but the final decision. She supposed that made him a free man. But the idea of her father dating would take some getting used to.

"Don't you ever eat Chinese food?" Anna asked her father as they sat down. She moved the vase of red roses so she could see his face. A Chinese waiter hovered behind them pouring wine and flipping serviettes.

"Oh yes, sometimes. But you know, honey, after living in China for three years you get a bit sick of it. Anyway, it's great having you here to stay. But we haven't seen each other much yet, have we? Haven't really had much of a chance to talk."

Anna gulped down a mouthful of red wine. She recognized the formal tone in her father's voice, the one he loved to use when lecturing her. She knew the conversation had to happen.

"So, have you decided what courses you're going to take next year? Your university application forms must be due soon."

The waiter presented them with menus and announced the specialities of the house. His accent was American, like that of a lot of young Chinese. They picked it up from CNN and Voice of America. Anna waited until he had gone.

"Well, I'm still quite keen on doing art, Dad," she began. Her first day at the college had reignited her passion.

Mr. White took a slow sip of wine and cleared his throat. "That's fine, darling," he said, "you can keep up with your painting on the weekends. But what are you going to study?"

"There are art courses I can do full time..."

Mr. White cut in before Anna could go on, "Look, Anna. You've already wasted one year. I'm not having you waste another.'

"But it's the only thing I really like to do." Anna's voice came out as a squeak.

Mr. White rested his elbows on the crisp white tablecloth and leaned toward her before speaking. "I know you think now that it would be a lot of fun to be an artist," —he made it sound like a dirty word—"but come on, be honest. You can't make money from art. How about doing an economics course and you can use your experience to do business with China?"

"I can't think of anything I'd like to do less!" she snapped, surprised at herself.

"Look, Anna, be realistic, we can't all do what we'd like to do!"

"Can't we?"

"No, of course not! Life is about compromise."

Anna felt edgy. She took another sip of red wine. She noticed through the wineglass how the candlelight made flickering red pools on the tablecloth. "Do you like what you're doing?"

Her father paused before he answered. "Yes, I suppose I do. You learn to like what you're doing. I came to China with nothing but a suitcase, but I'm earning good money now. I've built up my own business here in only three years. I own two apartments, I've put you girls through private school, and I expect to earn enough here in China to retire.

"I know it might all seem very confusing for you at the moment, honey, that's why you should take my advice. The trouble with your generation is they don't know where they are going. Kids your age are lost. They have too many choices. When I left school, there were only two options. You went to university or you got a job..."

Anna's mind began to wander. She had heard this lecture before. She thought about beautiful Chenxi and his magnificent painting. How was it that two people who grew up on opposite ends of the earth could have exactly the same vision? After what she had seen this afternoon it was impossible that they could not be together. She was sure he was the reason she came to China; everything happened for a reason.

Their waiter approached and Mr. White ordered quickly so he could continue, but Anna interrupted him before he could go on. "What do you think of Chenxi?" she dared.

Mr. White frowned. "I beg your pardon?"

"You know. The Chinese guy from my college."

"Have you been listening to me, Anna?" He stopped and eyed his daughter. "You don't have a crush on him, do you?"

"Maybe..." She twiddled her fork.

"Oh, Anna. You've only been here three days. You haven't been here long enough to understand."

"Understand what?"

"Look, love." His voice softened. "Chenksy seems like a very nice boy and I can certainly see how you're attracted to him, but just be careful."

"Dad!" Anna spluttered. "You're so patronizing! I know all about contraception and stuff like that, if that's what you mean. I'm not a virgin."

"That's *not* what I mean. Just be careful about what you get into. I know it sounds harsh, love, but a Chinese boy would do anything to go out with an American girl. You're probably lonely, but when I take you on Friday night for drinks at the consulate you'll meet some people you like. There are usually a few foreign students from the university up the road and from your art college. I've met a nice French boy who comes regularly. He's here studying Mandarin."

Anna stared at him. It struck her then that, despite living in China for three years, her father had no Chinese friends. He employed plenty of them—maids, drivers, even fellow engineers—but he didn't mix with them outside of work. Were all expatriates like that? She decided that in future she would keep her thoughts on Chenxi to herself.

In silence, Anna and her father ate their imported Italian meal and drank their imported red wine, the street sounds of Shanghai muffled by the altitude and the double-glazing of the top-floor restaurant.

FAR BELOW, along Zhong Shan Lu and past the street market, was the Shanghai College of Fine Arts. And, if you paused to look through the high iron gates, you might see a single bulb burning in the classroom on the second floor, where, having cooked for his mother, and after tucking the exhausted woman into bed, Chenxi sat meditating on his painting. A new painting he had just begun that evening. A painting of a girl.

On the other side of Shanghai, the subject of Chenxi's new painting sat down on her bed in the air-conditioned apartment that overlooked Fuxing Park. She took out her journal to gather her thoughts.

The next morning Anna arrived late at the college, hot and flustered, but proud she had negotiated her new pink bike through the traffic.

The other students were already at work, copying onto silk, and all of them looked up as she walked in, except Chenxi. Teacher Dai nodded and patted Anna's desk. Had he thought she wouldn't come back? The moon-faced boy beamed and slipped a note into Anna's hand as she walked past. She shoved it in her pocket.

Teacher Dai prodded Chenxi, who got up, making a performance of rinsing his brush and twisting the bristles into a fine point before ambling over to translate for Anna. She grinned at him and he returned a token smile.

"Teacher Dai say you can begin try bamboo today."

"Bamboo?" said Anna.

"Bamboo."

Anna stared at the newspaper laid out on her desk. Was she

not considered good enough to begin on rice paper?

Teacher Dai was looking back and forth between them, as if following a tennis match. When he saw Chenxi had finished translating, he nodded and smiled and took one of Anna's sheep-hair brushes from the bundle. He dipped it into a cup of warm water to soak out the protective glue and set about making ink for Anna.

Anna watched, fascinated, and Chenxi stood behind, translating whenever needed. Dai Laoshi rubbed the ink stick around and around the flat stone in a little water. Ink gradually formed from the powder dissolving into the liquid. He rubbed the stick almost meditatively, in rhythmic circles, then let Anna try.

Anna lost herself in the rhythm of the rubbing—what a calm beginning to a day's painting.

Once the ink was made and the brush soaked, Dai Laoshi dipped the tip of the bristles into the ink, instructing Anna not to have too much or too little. Then, with his arm curved loosely in front of him, the brush vertical, he let the tip down onto the newspaper, pushing the brush out in front of him.

"It important you paint with all your *chi*...your energy..." Chenxi translated, "not just you arm. *Chi* come from you stomach, run through you arm, through point of you brush. If you paint with *chi* you have good strong brush stoke."

Dai Laoshi lifted his brush, then pressed it down to form another stroke above the first. He looked at Anna to check that she was watching. Then he continued painting the same strokes until he reached the top of the newspaper.

"The stalk of bamboo," Chenxi announced.

With deft strokes, Dai Laoshi then painted the branches and the leaves of the bamboo, fanning out in orderly bunches of five. It looked easy. Deceptively so, as Anna discovered with her wobbly first attempt.

Chenxi and Dai Laoshi chuckled at the foreigner's bumbled effort, and Chenxi translated to Anna that she was to practice painting bamboos on newspaper at least until the end of the week.

"To the end of the week?" Anna frowned. She would rather be working on silk like the others.

Chenxi looked stern. "At least until end of week!"

Anna turned and began to paint another stalk of bamboo.

After her second hour of painting bamboos, with little improvement, she grew restless and gazed out the window. From where she sat she could see over to the bike shed where her bike shone out of the rusty tangle like an unwrapped candy. On the other side of the bike shed was another dull cement college building as formidable as a prison block, where row upon row of black heads were bent studiously over their work. She stretched and turned back to her class.

The moon-faced boy was looking at her and Anna remembered the note he had thrust in her hand. She took it out of her pocket and unfolded it. On the paper was a cartoon drawing of two lovebirds, and underneath he had written: *Hello! My name is Disco. Will you be my girlfriend?*

Anna giggled at the crazy name Moon-Face had chosen for himself. When she looked up he was grinning at her, his yellow teeth gleaming. She smiled and shook her head and Disco pulled an exaggerated grimace. Anna settled down to bamboo painting again, but felt her admirer watching.

At eleven twenty-five the students had already packed up, and at eleven-thirty most of them were out the door, caught up in the lunchtime mania. Disco straggled behind, lighting a cigarette and talking to Chenxi. Chenxi strolled over to Anna with Lao Li and Disco close behind, giggling and nudging each other like ten-year-olds.

Anna stood with her hands on her hips like a long-suffering primary school teacher, waiting for them to stop their silliness. Chenxi cocked his head, trying to suppress a smirk. "Ding Yue want to know why you not want to be his girlfriend?"

Anna rolled her eyes. "Ask Ding Yue why he calls himself Disco."

Chenxi translated Ding Yue's earnest response, his lips twisting in mirth. "He say he love disco and karaoke, and if you his girlfriend he take you to disco and karaoke bar his uncle own."

Lao Li shrieked with laughter.

"Well, tell Disco Ding Yue," said Anna, "that's it's fortunate I already have a boyfriend, because I hate disco and karaoke!"

Chenxi translated once again. Lao Li was laughing so hard he had tears in his eyes. Ding Yue clutched at his heart, pretending to be wounded, and dragged himself out of the classroom, howling all the way.

Anna turned to wash out her brushes, but Chenxi said, "Why you not want be girlfriend with Ding Yue, eh? His family own lot of factories. He make very good husband. Is because he Chinese?"

He watched for Anna's reaction.

Anna looked away and finished washing. "Of course not! I told you already! It's because I already love someone, OK? Are you coming for lunch, or what?"

She swung her bag over her shoulder and headed out of the room. Chenxi and Lao Li followed, Lao Li still hooting like a crazy animal.

THIS TIME AT THE NOODLE SHOP Anna was so hungry she decided to take the risk. She couldn't go to the Hilton for a hamburger every time she needed something to eat, and she felt like disobeying her father.

The three of them sat at a grimy table and the owner brought three bowls of soup noodles. Anna wiped her pair of chopsticks under the table on a clean tissue and, when nobody was looking, picked off the dried meat and flicked it to the floor, where it curled up into the dust. All that was left was a sprig of coriander, the noodles, and the soup. She hesitated for a minute, remembering her father's warning, but then told herself that she would rather be sick from tasting local food than return home healthy after only eating imported hamburgers.

The noodles were delicious. In fact they were so good that when Chenxi ordered a second bowl Anna did the same. This time she ate the whole lot, including the tasty dried meat, and when she sat back from the table, over-full and sweaty, she saw that Chenxi and Lao Li had been watching, impressed.

"What?" Anna snapped. "You think just because I'm a girl I can't eat as much as you?"

Chenxi chuckled and translated for Lao Li. Then he turned back to Anna and said, "That why Lao Li call you *Xiao Pang Pang*."

"What's that?" Anna said, pleased that she had already picked up a term of endearment for herself.

"It mean 'Small Fat Fat,'" Chenxi said, laughing.

Anna was mortified. "What?" she spluttered. "I'm not fat!"

"Yes you are!" said Chenxi. "In China to be fat is lucky. Lao Li think fat is beautiful."

Despite her liberal upbringing, Anna found it hard to take fat as a compliment! How different from her own culture's idea of beauty. Even she, despite being an average size, had succumbed to fetishes of dieting and starvation as a young teenager, like most of her friends at school.

She glanced at Chenxi slyly. "What about you? Do you like 'fat' girls?"

"I like all girls," he boasted, and Anna felt a tiny thread tighten inside her.

THAT AFTERNOON, the young model came to class again and smiled when she saw Anna. This time she undid her gown to the waist and sat stiffly, staring ahead of her as the class drew.

Anna took in her skeletal frame, small and neat like a child's. Her own body felt big and clumsy and the two bowls of noodles sat heavily in her stomach. But only that day, Anna reminded herself, she had been admired by two men, even if neither of them was Chenxi. Nevertheless, she was glad she was no longer a self-conscious schoolgirl who would have taken weeks to get over a remark like Chenxi's at lunchtime. It was like shaking off a cumbersome chrysalis to appreciate your body as it was. Anna smiled to herself as she drew.

Soon she felt Chenxi hovering behind her. Even though he didn't make a sound, she sensed an aura that sent her drawing arm to jelly. She put down her charcoal. The only way she could draw with him in the same room was to block him out of her mind. And that was no mean feat.

"Yes?" she said, turning to face him.

He smiled, stepping back.

Anna tried to think of something to keep his attention. "Chenxi," she whispered.

"Hmm?"

"You want to go for a swim this afternoon? In the consulate pool?" She hadn't even seen the pool, but she was sure it would entice him. "It's beautiful. And cool. And quiet. You know—tranquil?"

"Tranquil."

"Yes, tranquil. I taught you that word yesterday. Remember?"

"Tranquil. Calm. Yin and yang," Chenxi teased.

Anna reddened. "So. You want to come?"

"Maybe."

"What's that supposed to mean?"

Chenxi flicked through the small worn dictionary he carried in his pocket. "Maybe: perhaps, possibly..."

"Ha, ha, ha!" Anna said and went back to her drawing. "Come if you want. I don't care. I'm going anyway. It's too hot. I'll meet you at the American consulate at four."

FOUR O'CLOCK CAME AND WENT. Anna waited until ten past before diving into the pool. If he comes, he comes, she thought. I'm not going to hang around all day waiting for him again!

The cool, rippled turquoise closed over her. Underwater she could have been anywhere. But when she rolled onto her back and looked up at the gray polluted sky, she was unmistakably in Shanghai. Anna swam and dived and twisted through the water. Her pores were cleansed of the soot and silt but she could not rid her mind of Chenxi. Occasionally she felt sure of his presence and would flip over, certain he would be at the side of the pool, watching. But only the lush consulate palms waved back at her, and Anna tried to ignore her own disappointment.

After an hour, she got out of the pool and dressed, refreshed enough to feel herself again. She walked her bike out the front gate and was just about to mount when she heard Chenxi's call from behind.

"Chenxi! What are you doing here?"

"I wait for you!"

"But I've been here for ages! Why didn't you come in?"

"You tell me meet you at consulate. I wait here, outside."

"Oh, Chenxi! I feel terrible! I thought you weren't coming."

"I say only maybe. Maybe no. Maybe yes, too."

"Oh, I'm so sorry. Have you been waiting all this time? Come on, let's go for a swim now. I'll go in again."

"I must go help my mother cook dinner. She is home from work very tired."

"Chenxi, I really feel awful. How can I make up for it?" Anna searched his face to see if he was annoyed but she couldn't tell. "Look, I know. On Friday night they have drinks here, at the consulate. Would you come? At six?"

Chenxi stared across the road. "Maybe."

"Chenxi! Maybe yes, or maybe no?"

Chenxi winked. "Maybe. Perhaps. Possibly."

10

Lights sparkled and bobbed in the consulate pool. The sounds of forced laughter and the chinking of glasses wafted around the back porch of the old two-story mansion, along with the musky odor of perfume and sweat. Anna looked for Chenxi in case he had arrived early, but there were no Chinese in sight. The only Asian-looking man had a very strong American accent. Although it was evening and a breeze had lifted, all the foreigners had a sweaty sheen about them, as if they were in a state of constant anxiety. Some of the balding men carried monogrammed handkerchiefs, which they drew out of their top pockets from time to time to dab at their foreheads. Women slapped at mosquitoes around their bare ankles.

Anna was bored. She shifted from foot to foot half listening to the chatter around her. Why were they all here? What brought them to China? Living as an expatriate must be a bit like movie stardom in Hollywood. It was an unreal existence. Even though she complained about being stared at and touched in the streets, it was like being famous. A constant ego trip. Was that why all these foreigners were here? Were they nobodies in their own countries?

"Well, hello!" A woman in a cocktail dress and glittery nails floated toward her. "You must be Anna. Your father told me you were visiting. How are you enjoying it here?"

Anna didn't feel in the mood to play the good daughter. Her father spoke for her anyway, as she had expected he would, explaining that she was in China to "broaden her horizons" and to pick up a bit of Mandarin "to help her future career options." As Anna smiled distractedly, she kept a watch on the front gate. She had told Chenxi in the afternoon that if he was going to *maybe* come, then *maybe* he should come in. She couldn't wait for him all night out front.

A group of young people meandered through the gate, foreign students, and Anna's father nudged her. She looked them over perfunctorily and spied one who she guessed to be the French student her father was keen on. He had thick, curly brown hair, an attractive face, and was well dressed in cream linen pants and a silk shirt. But any interest she tried to summon up was banished by thoughts of Chenxi.

Anna excused herself from the conversation and wound her way through the sweaty bodies towards the trestle table set up as a bar. She jabbed a piece of cheese on the end of a toothpick and knew that she had been noticed. She picked up a flute of champagne and felt the French man sidle up behind her. He leaned in front of her to take a glass of beer, bumping her arm.

"Oh, excuse me!" he said in mock surprise.

Anna smiled, impressed at his smooth pick-up. He fitted her stereotype of a Frenchman.

"My name is Laurent. Are you a student here?" he continued without missing a beat.

"Anna. I'm studying Chinese painting at the Shanghai College of Fine Arts."

"Oh?" he said, feigning intense fascination. "You're an *artiste*!"

"I hope to be."

"I know that college. It's across the river from where I study at East China Normal University. I study Mandarin. You should come over and see us there one day." He gestured to include the other students he had arrived with. "We have great parties!"

"I should," Anna replied without promise and looked toward the front gate again. Chenxi was either very late or he wasn't coming.

Laurent noticed. "Are you waiting for someone?"

"Mmm," she nodded. "A classmate."

"Boy or girl?" he said with a teasing smile.

Anna decided that Chenxi wasn't coming. Anyway, it had been a while since she had played this game. It was a game she knew. With Chenxi she was never sure where she stood.

"Does it matter?" she said.

Laurent grinned, accepting his role. "That depends."

He took out a pack of Marlboros from his shirt pocket and offered her one. Anna knew smoking was about more than just cigarettes. It was a ritual, an ice breaker, an intimate little club. Chinese men never did deals without exchanging cigarettes. People who had never smoked didn't understand that in giving up smoking it wasn't the letting go of the cigarettes that was the hardest part.

"Smoke?"

"I've given up," said Anna regretfully.

"Shame," said Laurent. He flicked a match across a matchbook and held it to the cigarette hanging from his lips, his shoulders hunched up and his eyes squeezed. The flame created a little golden halo of light to frame his attractive face. He knew it.

Laurent puffed, shook the match out, and drew back deeply before fixing Anna's eyes. "What about hashish?"

"Well… I guess I'd give anything a try," Anna replied, hoping she sounded nonchalant.

Laurent smiled, delighted, and patted his trouser pocket. "Shall we go for a walk then?"

"I'll just tell my dad I'm getting a breath of fresh air. I'll meet you at the front gate," Anna said. Laurent didn't seem to worry about leaving the people he had come with.

Anna told her father she would find her own way home. He smiled approvingly in Laurent's direction and thrust some more notes into her hand.

"OK, love. You've got the spare key, haven't you? Have fun."

When Anna and Laurent reached the front gate of the consulate they heard a terrible commotion: angry voices and among them one Anna recognized. Chenxi! She pushed through the crowd and saw him arguing fiercely with the Consul guard. Every now and then Chenxi was interrupted as someone in the crowd offered their opinion. The guard was shaking his head.

"Chenxi!" Anna called. "What's the matter?"

Chenxi stopped shouting for a moment and looked at Anna. The crowd did the same. Then he turned back to the guard, pointing towards Anna, and continued shouting even louder.

"Is that your friend?" Laurent raised his eyebrows.

"Yes," said Anna.

"He's not acting very Chinese, is he?"

"What do you mean?"

"Well, he's saying some pretty heavy things for a Chinese. He should watch out. That kind of talk could get him into trouble."

Chenxi strode over. "He not want let me in. He say no Chinese allowed but I tell him you invite me," he muttered to Anna. "Shit!"

"We're leaving anyway," Anna said. "You want to come? This is Laurent."

Laurent slapped Chenxi amiably on the shoulder and said something long and complicated in Chinese. They both laughed.

"Yeah. I come," Chenxi said.

The three of them pushed through the arguing crowd and set off down the street.

Laurent and Chenxi chatted in Chinese as they strode through the pools of yellow light on the pavement. Anna followed and tried to look as if she didn't care that she couldn't understand.

Chenxi was warming to Laurent, and Anna wished yet again that she could speak Chinese. If there was a way to reach him it would certainly be through his own language. But we share a language, too. Our art. He has to feel there is some connection there. Surely the language of art traverses all cultures?

Laurent stopped and leaned against a high brick wall in the shadowy space between two streetlights. He took a film canister and a package of French cigarette papers out of his hip pocket.

Anna looked around. The street was certainly not empty. A sulky girl and her boyfriend walked past, turning to gape at the foreigners.

Laurent broke off a little of the greasy hashish and, with a practiced hand, mixed it with tobacco into one of the papers. Then he licked the seal and rolled a neat joint. Anna noticed that even though Laurent's hands were scrupulously clean, old stains of hashish had worked their way into his fingerprints.

"You're not going to light up here?" Anna said, astounded. A young man wobbled past on his bike, crooning to himself. An old lady stretched out of the window above, pulling her shutters closed, locking out the night. The streets were quiet in the consulate quarter, where the old European-style buildings and spotted plane trees lining the streets were reminiscent of France.

"They don't know what it is," Laurent assured her. "They

think it's just some strange type of foreign cigarette."

Anna had the feeling that Laurent might be showing off. For her benefit.

Laurent lit up and drew back hard, squinting in the smoke as he passed the joint to Anna. She took it and drew back tentatively at first, savoring the sweet musky taste. It was a lot stronger than grass. She handed the joint back to Laurent and waited for the effect.

Laurent offered the joint to Chenxi, who smiled slowly and shook his head. "I am Chinese, maybe, but I know what that is. I been to Xinjiang."

Laurent shrugged and took another drag.

Anna began to feel fuzzy. When Laurent passed the joint back to her, she drew on it again. Hard.

The street noises became treacly. The lights softened and blurred. Anna knew she was smiling like a fool.

They stood between two streetlights, against the brick wall.

Anna heard Laurent saying, "Hey, let's go to a bar!" His voice came to her as if through cotton batting.

She heard herself answer, "Sure."

"Do you have your bike?"

Anna thought for a while. "No."

"I take her on mine. It's in front of the consulate."

They walked back down the street to the front gate. Anna waited at the corner, worried that her father might appear. She wasn't sure if she was in a state to speak to him. Would he even recognize her? She felt sure she looked different. What did she look like?

After an eternity, Chenxi and Laurent returned on their bikes. Anna wanted to scold them for taking so long, but she couldn't find the words. Her voice seemed to be smothered with the same cotton wool.

ON THE BACK OF CHENXI'S BIKE, the ground whizzed beneath her. Too fast. If Anna looked up, the sinking starless sky made her feel worse. She concentrated on staring at Chenxi's arm.

She rested her cheek lightly against Chenxi's back, then withdrew it, suddenly not sure if it was Chenxi or Laurent. She studied the arm again and tried to tell by the color of the skin whose bike she was on, but the color seemed to change with every streetlight. She wondered how much longer it would be until they arrived. When they did, it seemed as if she'd only got on the bike, and she couldn't remember where they'd said they were going. She wanted to lie down.

CHENXI SMILED TO HIMSELF when he saw the same square man in the black suit at the door of the bar. His stance was the same as the other night, his arms crossed tightly. It was as if he hadn't moved. If the man recognized him, he made no sign of it, as Chenxi walked straight through the front door, a foreigner on either side of him. So, in your own country the worst racists are your fellow men, he thought bitterly.

11

Lying in her bed, listening to early morning waltzers in the park, Anna couldn't remember how she had got home. She remembered sitting in the bar drinking rum and Coke and then turning around to see that Chenxi had gone.

Laurent had kept her glass filled until suddenly Anna had felt a wave of nausea. A prickling on the insides of her cheeks. Laurent must have noticed her go pale because he took her outside. She remembered him standing a little way off, smoking a cigarette, while she retched into the bushes under the twinkly fairy lights. She thought she remembered a taxi.

Her father's alarm went off and Anna listened to the familiar shuffling of his morning ritual. Toilet. Shower. Shave. Breakfast. Teeth. She heard him tap on her bedroom door, and winced.

"Anna, I'm just going in to the office for a while. I'll be back for lunch. Are you feeling better?… Anna?… That nice French student who dropped you home last night told me it must have been the noodles you ate. Didn't I tell you not to eat in any local restaurants? You have enough money to eat out properly, don't you?... Honey?... I've left some more on the table just in case. If you're here when I get back for lunch we'll go out and get you a nice steak. I know a restaurant that imports them from Australia...Well, OK, honey. I'll ring from work if I get the chance. Don't forget, the *aiyi*'s coming today."

Anna lay quietly until she heard him close the front door. She found if she stayed very still she didn't feel so sick. When the waltzers had packed up and gone home, and all she could hear was the distant traffic, she drifted back to sleep.

She woke to the sound of the shower running. She looked down at her watch, but it was only ten-fifteen. Could her father be home early? She lay and listened. That was the sound of her hairdryer being used, and of someone scrabbling around in the bathroom cabinet. She lay still.

Her bedroom door opened and Anna quickly shut her eyes. The *aiyi*, a towel wrapped around her, wearing Anna's lipstick, gasped and made a hasty retreat. Anna heard her dressing in the bathroom.

A little while later, she heard the vacuum start, and the clunking of vases being dusted. She rolled over and took her journal out of the bedside drawer. Groaning, she heaved herself into a sitting position and waited for her head to catch up. Was it possible the hashish had made her so sick?

Anna gazed out through the window at the gray sky. Thoughts gathered in her head like shifting storm clouds. She heard the *aiyi* leaving. From below came the noise of the traffic and the ringing of bicycle bells. In her room it was air-conditioned and clean.

April 9th, 1989

Chenxi met me at the consulate last night. Well, out front anyway, but he came, so I am sure he must be interested in me. I met a French student, Laurent, good-looking but arrogant, who gave us some hashish to smoke. He told me he has a friend who travels regularly to Tibet to buy it, then Laurent sells it around his university campus. Chenxi knew what it was but he didn't smoke any. It made me sick.

By the time her father arrived home for lunch Anna was feeling better. Not quite well enough, however, to accept her father's offer of an Australian steak. Mr. White shrugged and made himself a cheese sandwich from a block of imported cheddar he fished out of the freezer and thawed in the microwave. Standing over the sink, his mouth crammed, he called to Anna, "How about getting outside for a while? It might make you feel better to get some fresh air."

"Fresh air?" Anna joked from her bedroom. The air in Shanghai was so fresh she could pick it in big black chunks out of her nose.

"Well, not literally speaking, I suppose. How about exercise then? We could catch a taxi and have a walk around the antique market. You haven't seen it yet, have you? It might be a good chance for you to pick up some souvenirs to take home."

"How about riding our bikes, if you really want some exercise?"

"Oh, it's too much hassle to get them out of the shed, honey. Besides I think mine has a puncture."

Anna heard him slap the crumbs off his hands and then step into the lounge room. "It only costs one yuan to get a puncture fixed, Dad. That's twenty-five cents."

"Really?" Mr. White mumbled, mostly to himself. "They always charge me ten yuan!"

Anna emerged from her bedroom, buttoning her shirt and grinning. She poked her father in the ribs. "That's because you're a foreigner, Dad!"

"A *wai guo ren*," Mr. White chuckled, in a strong American accent.

"A long nose."

"A foreign ghost."

"A cheese-smelling, FEC-spending, foreign devil!"

"That's going too far!" Mr. White laughed. "Come on, let's go out and spend some of this filthy FEC that the Chinese seem to want so much!" He linked his arm in Anna's.

"Hey, Dad? I've written some postcards home. Can we stop on the way to send them?"

"Just leave them on the chair by the door for the *aiyi*," Mr. White said. "She'll do it. I have to warn you though, the postal service is unreliable. You might get home before your cards do. We can give your mother a call tonight, if you like. If you want to speak to your sisters."

"Nah, it's fine," Anna said. "I've only been away a few days.

They'll be fine. Maybe next week."

Mr. White squeezed his daughter's shoulder in a sudden burst of affection.

ON A WORN STRAW MAT, a peasant girl laid out her meager wares. She had traveled for two days to reach Shanghai, leaving her elderly grandmother in the care of her neighbor. She would not make much money that day but, since her mother had died and her grandmother was ill, any extra money for the doctor's fees would help.

She unwrapped the last item, hesitating before she placed it among the other objects on the mat. It was a silver snuffbox inlaid with precious stones, dating from the Ching dynasty and handed down from mother to eldest daughter over many generations. Today would be the day it left the family, the peasant girl thought wistfully. She thanked the spirits her grandmother was blind and wouldn't notice its absence.

Her neighbor, who had been to Shanghai before, told the girl the snuffbox was worth a lot of money. She should ask for two hundred yuan and accept nothing less than a hundred. One hundred yuan! That was more money than she earned in two months!

Crowds shuffled past. Occasionally they turned the peasant girl's items over and one of them even picked up the snuffbox and asked its price. When she told the man he snorted and walked off.

As the morning slipped by, the girl began to worry. What if she didn't make enough to cover her train fare? Could she dare return home without a coin? She crouched on her haunches, squinting up at the bustling people.

Eventually, a young foreign woman, wearing shorts and a t-shirt, paused at the girl's mat. She glanced over the objects while the peasant girl gazed up at her, dazzled by the foreigner's white skin and blue eyes. Before Anna had the chance to slide back into the crowd, the young girl snatched up the bejeweled snuffbox and thrust it into her hand.

Anna smiled and placed the tiny box back on the mat. "No, thanks," she said.

Her eyes wild, the peasant girl shook her head and pushed the box back into Anna's hand and held two fingers up at her face.

"Two yuan?" Anna guessed without a clue. "*Liang kuai?*"

The girl shook her hands frantically and scribbled two, zero, zero on a scrap of paper. She held it up for Anna to see. Anna was examining the pretty box.

"Oh, two hundred," Anna said. "*Liang bai?*"

The peasant girl nodded.

"No thanks," Anna said and made to walk off.

It was nearly the end of the day and the peasant girl hadn't sold a thing. At home her grandmother lay waiting in the darkness of their hut. The girl stepped forward in a panic and grabbed at the foreign girl's sleeve before she disappeared. This was her last chance.

Anna spun around.

"*Yi bai wu shi kuai! Yi bai wu shi!*" the peasant girl cried.

"No, really," Anna said. "Even for a hundred and fifty, I don't want it."

Anna's father pushed through the small crowd that had gathered. "What's going on?" he said.

"She wants me to buy her box." Anna was agitated now. The peasant girl thrust the box at Mr. White. He inspected it, frowning.

"Hmm…" he said. "It looks quite valuable."

"Ching Dynasty," a spectator confirmed.

"But I don't want it!" Anna insisted.

"*Yi bai! Yi bai kuai!*" the peasant girl cried.

"Mmm. One hundred yuan she's asking for it," said Mr. White. "But you should always bargain them down to half price. As you know they think we are full of money and they'll always try to cheat us.

"Fifty!" he said loudly to the peasant girl. "*Wu shi yuan!*"

The peasant girl was horrified. She shook her head savagely and grabbed the box. Mr. White shrugged and turned his back to her. The crowd chuckled.

"She'll come after us," he whispered.

Sure enough, just as they began to walk away, the peasant girl took hold of Anna's arm again, and stared at her with pleading eyes. "*Ba shi*," she said. "*Ba shi! Ba shi!*" She took both of Anna's hands in her own, the precious box sealed between them.

"No!" Mr. White looked fierce and shook his head. "Not eighty! Fifty!"

"Dad! I don't want it!"

Mr. White tried to pull his daughter from the peasant girl's grasp. The crowd pressed in around the spectacle.

"*Wu shi!*" the peasant girl wailed, holding tight. "*Wu shi! Wu shi! Wu shi!*"

"Dad!"

Mr. White peeled off crisp notes from the stack in his wallet. Two twenties and a ten. He thrust the bright money into the dark hand and snatched the silver box.

The peasant girl looked down at the unfamiliar notes in her trembling hands. When she lifted her head, the foreigners had gone and the little crowd had dispersed. She shuffled back to her mat to find that a jade pendant had been stolen.

In the rear seat of the air-conditioned taxi, Anna was miserable. She looked down at the little silver box. When she opened the lid a faint musty smell came out, and on the base, in a shaky hand, a Chinese character had been carved.

"That was a good find, Anna," her father said, satisfied, from the front seat. "That box would be worth at least five hundred yuan in an antique store!"

Anna sighed, and knew why she didn't feel elated. She saw herself in Chenxi's eyes: the privileged foreigner with an endless supply of FEC and wondered if his ambivalence toward her was more about what she stood for rather than who she was. She would prove to him that she was different from other foreigners. She was not a rich and greedy capitalist like the other expatriates here seemed to be—she was an artist. Like him. She would show him that they had more in common than their differences.

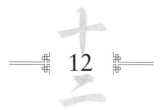

12

On Monday, Anna arrived at the college to find it deserted. Annoyed at not being informed of whatever public holiday it was, she was about to leave when she saw the director's secretary walking from the canteen to the main college building. Anna rode up behind her. The secretary turned but, when she saw who it was, her face clouded with a look of irritation.

"Miss Anna!"

"Where is everyone?"

"No school," the secretary snapped. "How you say?... Study from nature. All students traveling for two weeks, leaving tomorrow. What you want to do? You want me organize you private teacher teach you at home?"

"Well, I'd like to have gone with my class!" Anna grumbled. "After all, I am a student here, too, aren't I?"

The secretary took a deep breath. "Come with me."

Anna chained her bike to the empty rack and followed her to the director's office.

THE DIRECTOR WAS EVEN LESS PLEASED to see his foreign student. Anna could imagine him wondering if the special high fees her father was paying were worth the trouble she was causing.

His secretary explained the situation and they argued back and forth for a while, jabbing at maps and calendars. At one point Anna recognized Chenxi's name and even though she was sorry for pulling him into her problems again she was relieved that he might be looking after her. She couldn't bear the idea of two weeks in Shanghai without him.

The director picked up the telephone and asked for Chenxi. He waited a long time, tapping his pen impatiently, but when Chenxi came on the line the conversation was brief.

The director hung up and leaned back in his chair. The secretary took Anna's hand in both of hers and said, "Chenxi coming."

Anna relaxed. A class excursion with Chenxi! The three of them sat in silence, not looking at each other, until Chenxi arrived ten minutes later.

"Hi," Anna offered meekly.

Chenxi gave her a thin smile, but wouldn't meet her eye.

The director barked out a few commands and Chenxi nodded.

"You go with Chenxi," the secretary said. She and the director stood up and waited for Anna and Chenxi to leave.

OUTSIDE, ASTRIDE HER BIKE, Anna tried to start a conversation with Chenxi. He was unlocking his bicycle from the rack and still wouldn't look at her. "Where are we going?" she asked sweetly.

Chenxi slid his leg over the seat of his old brown bike and pushed down on the pedal. Anna followed him out of the college grounds on her candy-pink bike.

"I not know," he grumbled.

"What do you mean?" Anna asked. "Aren't we going on an excursion with our class?"

He shook his head. "Not for foreigners."

"What?"

"Tomorrow my class travel south visit minority group for drawing them. This region is not allowed for foreigners. We must go to different place."

"No foreigners?"

He nodded. "Closed to foreigners."

"But that's crazy!" Anna objected. She had heard of Chinese people not being allowed into certain places where foreigners could go, but she had never known that there were places that foreigners couldn't access. It shouldn't be allowed! "But, why?"

Chenxi shrugged. "There are some places Chinese government do not like foreigners see. Chinese government only like foreigners see pretty places where there no troubles. Then foreigners go home to their country and tell everyone what lovely peaceful country is China."

Chenxi sped up to pass a slowing bus. Anna fell behind and was accosted by a young man with thick glasses who rode alongside her shouting, "Hello! Hello!" She pushed harder on her pedals to catch up with Chenxi.

Anna reached him, out of breath. It annoyed her that Chenxi always rode so fast. "Look, I'm sorry! I didn't know," she panted. She had caused problems for Chenxi again. "I'll just stay home for two weeks. That's OK. You can't miss out on this trip with your class. You go. I'll just stay at home. The secretary said she could organize a teacher for me at the apartment. Don't worry about me."

Still not turning even to glance at her, Chenxi shook his head. "The director say I look after you."

"Don't worry. I won't tell him. He won't find out. What he doesn't know won't hurt him, hey?"

"Oh, they know, they know. They find out. You must come with me. I already think where we can go. We can visit my sister. She live in Shendong, near Xian. She has two boy. I do not see them very long time."

Anna realized they were riding toward her apartment.

"Sorry," she said again, chewing the inside of her lip.

Chenxi didn't reply.

THEY RODE SIDE BY SIDE down Huai Hai Lu, the road that had become almost as familiar to Anna as her street back in San Francisco. She recognized all the stores now. The fashion shops with their window displays of dusty blouses, the grocery stores, and the medicine shops full of curious dried herbs and animal parts. She had been in Shanghai a week. Sometimes it felt like she had arrived only yesterday, but most of the time it felt much longer.

At times she couldn't imagine her life before Chenxi; he was always on her mind. California, and the life she had left behind, seemed like a distant planet. The couple of times she had spoken to her friends or her sisters on the phone, they were caught up in the same trivial problems as when she had left and she found it hard to reconnect with them. She felt changed. Different. Chenxi was her delicious secret. She didn't think they would understand her obsession with him. She could barely understand it herself.

Apart from that one enlightening moment in the classroom when they had discussed the painting, Anna still felt no closer to Chenxi. It seemed the more time she spent with him the less she knew him. The more distant and aloof he was with her, the more desperately she wanted to understand him. Just to know that she might be special for him. She couldn't bear to think that he might not feel anything for her. Perhaps seeing him with his family would give her the chance she needed.

They turned into her street. To her surprise, when Anna asked him up to the apartment to discuss their trip, Chenxi accepted.

The sentry peered out of his box suspiciously as Chenxi pedaled past.

"Can I get you some tea? Sit down," Anna said. Chenxi was standing by the sitting room window that overlooked the front gate.

He turned, startled. "Yes. OK. Tea. Green tea?"

"No, just English Breakfast," Anna said. "Sorry."

She bustled around in the kitchen putting cookies on a plate. "What did you do on the weekend?" she called out, desperate to make conversation. Was that the type of thing Chinese people asked?

"I go to college for paint," Chenxi replied.

"Really?" Anna walked into the sitting room and put the cookies on the coffee table. Chenxi took three. "You paint on weekends?"

"Every weekend," mumbled Chenxi with his mouth full. He picked up another cookie and turned it over to inspect it. "It has good taste."

"Have another," Anna said, pushing the plate toward him. "What are you painting? Are you still working on the same piece?"

Chenxi brushed the sugar off his hands and sat down on the couch. He took a crumpled pack of cigarettes from his top pocket. "No. That painting finished." He glanced across at Anna and smiled. "I dark the front bit like you say. It much better now. Thank you." He took a cigarette out of the pack and tapped it a few times on the box.

Anna walked across the room to open the window. "It's always easier to talk about other people's work than your own."

"Yes. But no person talk about my work before. No one here understand my work."

"Really?" Anna said, shocked. She came to sit by Chenxi. "I would have thought it spoke for itself. To me it's very clear."

"Yes. But you see already what we must paint in class. That is type of painting accepted in China. What I paint is too different. You think people understand my painting in America?"

"Of course! It's fantastic! I know a few galleries that would exhibit your work straight off!" Anna boasted. "One at least, for sure. The owner is a friend of the family. I've had an exhibition there already. Well, I had a piece in an exhibition."

"Really?" Anna had Chenxi's full attention now. "You sell it?"

"I didn't show it to sell. But you could sell yours."

"Really? How much?"

"Oh, I don't know… A thousand dollars or more for the big one… I've no idea."

"American dollars? One thousand American dollars?"

"I'm not sure, Chenxi. I'm just taking a wild guess." Anna shifted uncomfortably. The kettle whistled and she stood, relieved that she could unfasten herself from this unexpected attention. Chenxi leaned back into the couch and lit his cigarette.

In the kitchen Anna poured the boiling water into the pot. She was feeling anxious. The questions Chenxi asked were perfectly valid, but she had hoped he wouldn't be interested in money the way everybody else was. For her, discussing art and money was sacrilegious. But was she being unrealistic? Perhaps she could only afford the luxury of not being interested in money because she had never had to worry about it.

Anna carried the tea tray out to the sitting room. "I've got a map of China in my bag,' she said to change the subject. "Can you show me where we're going?"

Chenxi was lounging back with his feet on the coffee table, meditating on the blue smoke drifting above his head.

"Chenxi?" Anna said. "Can you show me where your family lives?" She spread her map out on the coffee table. Chenxi swung his feet to the floor and peered at the Chinese characters.

"Here," he said. "See, this where my family live. Shendong. Near Xian."

"Is that where your parents are from?"

"My mother only," Chenxi said. "She move to Shanghai when she finish school."

"And what about your father?" Anna asked. "What does he do? Is he an artist like you?"

"I have no father," Chenxi said.

"Oh, I'm sorry. Is he dead?" Anna said, embarrassed, but curious.

"I have no father like you have no mother."

"Oh, I have a mother. She's back home with my sisters. My parents don't live together. They're separated. Is that what happened to your parents? Are they divorced?"

"Divorce is what foreigners do," Chenxi said. "Not Chinese." He stood up and walked over to the window to signal that it was the end of the conversation.

Anna poured herself another cup of tea. She tried to think of something she could say to him that would open him up again. She always seemed to say the wrong thing. Asked too many questions. She would have to learn to be more careful.

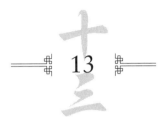

13

On China Airlines to Xian the cabin crew hung around the front of the plane chatting and threw boxes of fruit juice to any passengers who dared complain. Everything was so makeshift, it felt to Anna as if the plane were sticky-taped together. When she put her hand up to the scratched plastic window, she could feel the air that whistled through the seals.

By twisting the facts Anna had managed to convince her father to let her go on the trip. She hadn't told him she would be traveling alone with Chenxi. He was led to believe she was going on a college art excursion and Mr. White had agreed to let her go on the condition that she fly rather than take the train. If she took the twenty-seven-hour train trip, he was sure she would arrive ill. What with all the inedible food and the state of the railway toilets, she would be much better off to let her class settle in for the first week and join them on the weekend. A week would be plenty of time away, he assured her.

So Chenxi left on the Tuesday by train and Anna flew to join him on Saturday.

As the plane descended into Xian Airport, the passengers were already standing, pushing and shoving by the doors before the aircraft had landed. The cabin crew called out in Chinese, then English: "All passengers to return to their seats." Only one or two obeyed.

When the doors were unbolted, the crew flattened themselves against the walls as the surge of people rushed to be first off. Thinking there must be a reason for the panic, Anna dived into the crowd and let herself be swept along.

When she surfaced again she found herself in a dusty tin shed. In the center was an enormous pile of suitcases. Passengers were clambering over it to find their possessions and Anna was thankful she'd carried everything in her backpack as carry-on luggage.

She looked for an exit and saw that the far wall of the shed was constructed with chicken wire, behind which another crowd was scrambling, searching for their loved ones. Anna was thankful to see Chenxi. He called her over and laughed when he saw her worried face. "Come on," he said, swinging her bag over his shoulder. "We must get bus. Two bus."

Chenxi seemed pleased to see her. Anna jogged to keep up with him as they headed out of the parking lot, away from the crowds and haggling taxi drivers. Their steps made balloons of dust.

During the long walk down the airport driveway, no one passed them. It was weirdly quiet and sunny after the pollution of Shanghai. Anna could even hear birds chirping. It was peaceful trotting along behind Chenxi and she had the urge to take his arm in hers. But she contented herself with his closeness.

A cyclist approached, wobbling under a bulky load, as if drunk. As he came closer, his dirt-streaked brow furrowed in concentration, Anna saw that he had slung the carcass of an enormous pig over the back of his bike. The head of the pig gazed glassily from the basket on the front. The cyclist gawked at Anna. His bike leaned dangerously and the hoofs of the pig scratched little trails in the dust. Anna giggled, and skipped to catch up with Chenxi.

They arrived at their stop just as the bus pulled to a halt. Chenxi pushed Anna up the steps, swinging in behind her. She squeezed into a seat and held on as the bus bumped and churned along.

Gray buildings like cement shoe boxes clustered closer together, and more and more cyclists appeared as they drew into the center of Xian.

THE CITY WAS SHABBIER and dustier than Shanghai, but its streets weren't as crowded. Anna held tight to the tail of Chenxi's shirt for fear of losing him as he jostled through the people who stopped in mid-stride to stare at them both. Every few minutes, Chenxi turned to see what was keeping Anna, and she bumped into him. But most of the time she kept her head down and tried to avoid getting caught in the grasp of the beggar children clutching at her.

"Xian have many robbers," Chenxi whispered as they boarded the next bus. "Be careful your money! They see foreigner — watch out!"

This time they had no room to sit, so Anna held on to a leather strap suspended from the ceiling. By her side stood a young peasant man with hair slicked across his forehead and strappy plastic sandals. His hands were rough and nicotine-stained and, as Anna watched him, he slipped one of them into her jacket pocket.

"Can you take your hand out of my pocket, please?" she said politely, as she stared at him in shock.

He looked up at her, then continued to rustle around among the dirty tissues. Anna tried to think of the words in Chinese, but all she managed was, "No! No good!"

Undeterred, the man took his hand out of her left pocket and slipped his arm around her waist to try his luck in the other one. Anna almost laughed. She didn't really want to get him in trouble, but she wondered if he was going to work his way down her trousers to where her money was really stashed. So she hissed to Chenxi, who was a little way down the bus, "Hey, Chenxi, how do you say in Chinese, 'Stop thief!'"

He looked at her, puzzled.

"There's a man who keeps putting his hand in my pockets!"

Chenxi shouted something in Chinese and suddenly there was an uproar. The bus screeched to a halt in the middle of the road and a pack of squealing housewives threw the young thief off the bus, clucking in disapproval and shaking their heads as the doors closed again. The bus started up and as Anna watched him slink off down the footpath, she felt sorry for the simple young man.

THE CROWD ON THE BUS thinned out eventually and Anna slipped into a seat by the window. She was hot and sticky, but she kept her jacket on for fear of losing it to another pair of nifty hands.

Out the window she watched as a larger bus, even more dilapidated than theirs, rumbled by with dozens of squawking and flapping chickens strapped to the roof. A peasant squatted in the shade of his doorway, which was hung with bright cobs of drying corn. Women trotted by, balancing heavy baskets hung on springy bamboo poles over their shoulders. Everyone who noticed Anna's fair face peering from the bus window stopped and stared.

Chenxi slid in next to Anna and said, "It is very far place."

Anna watched the flat patchwork countryside spinning by outside the open window. Within minutes she had dozed off, her head on Chenxi's shoulder.

Chenxi didn't move for the remainder of the forty-minute ride.

A TALL WOMAN WAS WAITING at the only bus stop in Shendong, with a skinny young boy in thongs twisting around her legs. She smiled when Anna stepped off the bus and took both her hands in her own. She had Chenxi's smile, but her eyes smiled too, wrinkling at the edges. Anna suspected she was older than she looked.

It was impossible to read the age of Chinese people: an old man had once approached Anna in the street and asked her in perfect English to guess his age. Anna said fifty, guessing sixty, and was astounded to discover he was eighty-seven! He had ridden off, chortling in satisfaction.

"Your sister?" Anna asked.

"The small sister of my mother. I have no brother or sister."

"She's called your aunt, then."

Chenxi introduced them rapidly: the woman's name was Yang Wen and the gawky boy, in his last year of primary school, was Zhou Jin. As they began to walk, Chenxi explained to Anna that Chinese women kept their maiden names which was why his aunt's family name Yang was different from her son's. The children automatically took their father's name.

The four of them had only gone a little way down the street before Yang Wen stopped in front of a photo-processing shop and muttered something shyly to Chenxi. Chenxi sighed and said, "My sister want to show you some people."

"Aunt," Anna corrected. "Of course."

They filed into the small shop and a smirking fat man with greasy hair came from behind the counter to meet them.

"Oh!" he said, nodding and smiling at Anna. "America,

America." Obviously he had been expecting her.

"Yes," said Anna.

"Very good! Very good!" The man put both his thumbs up.

He found a few stools for them and they sat down to talk, everyone looking over at Anna as if to include her. Chenxi was standing by the wall, studying a calendar, so Anna didn't ask him to translate.

Twenty minutes later they stood up to leave, and bade the man farewell. Out in the street, only a short distance on, Chenxi's aunt made the same request, except this time it was to meet the owner of the grocery store.

Nearly two hours later, having been presented to every shop owner and postal clerk in the town of Shendong, the four of them reached Yang Wen's home. Anna was exhausted after being poked and prodded like a prize pony. But, just when she thought the parade was over, waiting for them in the family's little room was the other half of the town!

The round rosewood table was littered with peanut shells and mandarin skins; people were perched on stools and on the edge of the big bed, smoking and chatting. They had clearly been there for some time.

"Aah!" they cried in delight as Anna walked in. They busied about, finding her a stool, and passing her tea and nuts and fruit. Anna tried to catch Chenxi's eye, but he was concentrating on peeling a mandarin.

One by one the visitors left, and Chenxi introduced Anna to the remainder of his aunt's family. Yang Wen's husband was tall with a wide nose and thick glasses. His name was Zhou Yi and he too gave Anna a warm welcome. Their eldest son, who was fifteen, had his father's nose and bad vision. He introduced himself to Anna in faltering English as Zhou Lai, and everybody laughed good-naturedly. He went on to say that he was studying English at school and happy to have someone to practice with. Lastly, the ancient lady with the golden rings in her long, dark earlobes was his uncle's mother. But Anna could call her *Nai nai*, which meant grandmother. This made everybody laugh again.

Anna handed Chenxi's aunt the box of chocolates she had brought. The aunt smiled and thanked Anna, then placed them in a cupboard next to two other unopened boxes of chocolates.

Chenxi's uncle slapped his thigh and rummaged around in his vinyl satchel to pull out a camera. They took turns in taking photos and sitting next to Anna. Then Chenxi's aunt dashed out to call a neighbor to take a photo of the whole family. They cheered as the flash went off, then sat the neighbor down with Anna and took a last photo of the two of them. Anna's cheeks ached from smiling.

Soon after it was time to eat. Chenxi helped his grandmother and aunt cook in a wok on a coal burner just outside the doorway. Anna offered to help, but Chenxi's aunt looked offended. Chenxi explained that his aunt was perfectly able to cook by herself and didn't require any help from a guest, thank you very much! So Anna sat and waited to be fed, embarrassed to have assumed the manners she had been brought up with would be relevant in China.

Zhou Jin and his father brought in the dishes as they were

cooked and set them in front of Anna with great ceremony. Zhou Lai sat next to her on the bed and tried to explain in English what was in them.

"Beans. Fish. Pig. That one is...how you say... *doufu*?"

"Tofu."

"*Doufu* in hot sauce. That one is," — he flicked through a dictionary — "tongue from duck."

"Duck?"

"Quack? Quack?"

"Yes, it's duck."

The tongues were longer than Anna had expected, but she had never really thought much about that part of the bird's anatomy.

She was surprised at how delicious the food was. She tasted everything except the duck tongues. This omission seemed to disappoint the family: it was clear they had ordered the delicacy especially for her.

Instead of eating over a bowl of rice, as was the custom in Shanghai, they picked the food directly from the dishes with their chopsticks and ate over a steamed rice-flour bun, called a *mantou*, which also served as a plate. Any dish that Anna showed a liking for was pushed in front of her, while Chenxi's nephew laughed as he translated, "You like? You eat all!"

Chenxi didn't speak much, except to correct Zhou Lai's translations, but he appeared relaxed with his family. At the end of the meal, he shared cigarettes at the table with his uncle, and the two boys joked with Anna while their mother and grandmother washed up. Night had fallen and, when Anna yawned, Chenxi's uncle jumped up and called to his wife, who rushed in wiping her hands on her apron.

Yang Wen linked Anna's arm in hers and took her across to the four-story concrete building opposite the one-roomed apartment where they had been eating. She called for Chenxi to follow with Anna's bag. They crossed the dusty courtyard, then walked up a dimly lit stairwell to the second floor, and along a corridor smelling of fish and steamed rice. Anna heard the clicking of chopsticks in ceramic bowls as other families chatted or ate.

At the end of the corridor, Yang Wen pulled a key out of her pocket and unlocked a door onto a small bedroom with a clean cement floor. Yang Wen turned on the lights, then the television, and all the family came up to sit with Anna. They cracked pumpkin seeds with their teeth and watched the news together.

Anna looked around the little room bathed in fluorescent light and thought how simple and uncluttered it was. Everything was neatly arranged. She recalled the rambling old house she lived in with her mother and sisters in an affluent neighborhood of San Francisco, and the things they had accumulated over the years. Every time they moved to a bigger house, it was only to fill it with more mess.

When the news finished, Yang Wen shooed the men out of the room, and Chenxi explained to Anna that she would sleep with his aunt. His uncle, his nephews, and he would share the room opposite. His grandmother would sleep as she always did, in the room where they had eaten.

Anna undressed as Yang Wen swept the floor, which was now littered with cigarette butts and pumpkin seed husks. Then Yang Wen unrolled a padded silk quilt embroidered with peonies and tucked it around Anna like a sleeping bag. As she chatted to Anna in Chinese, she slipped off her clothes, down to her underwear, and slid into another quilt beside Anna.

Anna moved her head around to make a dent in the crunchy pillow that seemed to be filled with sand or chaff. But it stayed solid and her squirming only served to unwrap the quilt. So she wriggled off the pillow down into the bed, and fell asleep.

14

When Anna woke, she was alone. Judging by the pale light slanting in at the window it could not have been very late, but the other half of the bed was already made up, the thick quilt rolled at the end. She considered turning over and going back to sleep, but remembered she was a guest and slunk out of bed.

Though sunny, it was surprisingly cool. She put on her jacket over the long t-shirt she had slept in and rummaged in her bag for a pair of leggings. When she was dressed she walked over to the window to find her bearings.

The glass was covered with a thin film of dust. Even if you did have an *aiyi* come three times a week, as her father did, dust was something impossible to remove in China. Everything was covered in it. She swung the window open and looked down onto the room where they had dined the night before. Anna watched Yang Wen and her mother-in-law squatting outside, talking as they scraped vegetables. Chenxi stood at the cement trough, in his cargo pants and a tank top, his shirt tied around his waist. He was brushing his teeth. In the morning light his skin gleamed golden over the muscles in his back.

Chenxi's eldest nephew, Zhou Lai, was the first to spot Anna spying from above. "Good morning!" he called out, pleased to be the first to speak with her.

The family looked up at Anna. She tried her faltering Chinese for the attentive audience, "*Ni hao!*"

They all roared in appreciation.

"Come down, sleepy mouse!" Chenxi smiled up at her. "Your breakfast is soon cold."

THEY FED ANNA rice porridge with sugar, and fried dough sticks. When she had eaten her fill, she asked, "Where is the shower?" and watched Chenxi's face fall. He whispered to his aunt who shook her head before replying. Chenxi translated, "My aunt take you now."

Yang Wen disappeared and came back with a towel and a pair of plastic thongs for Anna, soap in a plastic container, and a bottle of shampoo. The shower must be communal, Anna guessed. That's what they were worried about! But she didn't mind at all.

Anna was obliged to guess again when Yang Wen beckoned her out the front gate and down the street. They walked for a few minutes, waving at everyone Yang Wen knew, until they came to a shabby hotel.

In the foyer, Yang Wen paid a few coins to a bored woman at reception and received a couple of plastic tokens. They made their way out the back through another door and down the side of the hotel. Here, the passageway opened into a small courtyard and another woman behind a desk took the plastic tokens. When she spied Anna behind Yang Wen, she called out. A woman appeared from behind steamy glass doors to stare at the foreigner. Anna looked at Yang Wen to see what was expected of her now.

FIVE MINUTES LATER Anna found herself wearing only her plastic thongs and standing among a dozen other naked women. They all stared at her. She turned the tap and a jet of lukewarm water cascaded out from a nozzle in the wall. There was only one temperature. Anna closed her eyes and leaned into the torrent, listening to the murmur of "*Wai guo ren! Wai guo ren!*"

When she opened her eyes, she found a woman right up close, staring at her, mouth agape. Anna nodded with an awkward smile. This seemed to break the trance and one by one the women went back to scrubbing each other's backs, only glancing at Anna occasionally.

She scrubbed herself for what she thought would be at least three days' worth and dressed quickly to find Yang Wen, who was waiting outside.

THE DAYS ANNA SPENT in the town of Shendong passed quickly. In the mornings, she added to her journal or wandered around the streets. After an early lunch, she and Chenxi hopped on bikes and rode out into the countryside to draw from nature. Sometimes they spent the whole afternoon studying the changing light on a haystack; other afternoons they sat and sketched a busy marketplace. When they were on their own Chenxi began to relax, and a couple of times—to Anna's delight and his dismay—she caught him making sketches of her. But he always refused to let her see them.

Sometimes he studied a drawing she was working on, or asked advice about composition. It wasn't that she was necessarily the better artist, Anna reflected modestly, but she had a freedom and a fluidity that she could see Chenxi envied. He was amazed, once, to watch her, when she was in an experimental mood, elongate the already long chin of an old man snoozing. On its own it would have seemed ridiculous, but in the context it seemed to describe the sleepy feel of the old man better than Chenxi's perfectly proportioned portrait.

"Can you do that at your school?" he asked.

"Chenxi, this is art!" Anna boasted. "You can do what you want!"

He nodded to himself, frowning.

Out of the corner of her eye Anna could see Chenxi watching her. She put down her pencil. "You know what I think?" she said, feeling confident. "I think an artist's responsibility is to show a different world to the viewer. No, not a different world," she corrected herself, working on her theory as it came to her, "the same world, but a different way of looking at it."

Chenxi was busy sketching the landscape, but Anna could tell he was listening. She went on. "It is an artist's responsibility, and I'm talking about writers and musicians too, to take the smaller paths that come off the main road. To go down them and to bring back what they find for those people who never dare to go themselves. Or never have the chance."

Anna took out a fresh piece of paper and brushed her hand across it. She squinted at the tip of her pencil. "You know, if I painted one painting that changed the life of one person, affecting them deeply enough to make them see something in a completely different way—even if only one person—I feel like I would have achieved something. My father doesn't understand that. For him, if it doesn't make money it doesn't count."

"You can think like that because you're free," Chenxi mumbled.

"What did you say?"

But Chenxi stood up without answering and moved away to begin another drawing.

ONE AFTERNOON, at the end of the week, they were in a field when the wind blew up and the air grew cool. Chenxi wanted to take Anna home, but she scoffed, not wanting anything to shorten her time alone with him. She insisted that they stay.

It was Chenxi's turn to be triumphant, when, back at his aunt's home, Anna began to sneeze and shiver. His aunt, her face pale, put Anna straight to bed and brought a bowl of steaming chicken's feet soup.

When Anna came down with a fever, they called the local doctor, despite her protestations. He tutted and shook his head and prescribed a dozen foul-smelling dried herbs and some tiny white pills in a paper package. Anna swallowed the pills and pinched her nose to drink the even fouler tasting brew that Yang Wen concocted from the herbs. Chenxi sat by her bed that afternoon and Yang Wen slept with her at night.

The following day, when she woke from a light sleep, Anna found Chenxi gazing down at her. She saw the anxiety in his eyes. He looked away, but she didn't want to let the opportunity slip. She had seen something there.

"You're worried about me!" she joked. "I've only got a cold, for God's sake! Do you think I'm going to die on you or something?"

Chenxi told her off: "You think it funny, huh? My aunt worry all the time. If something happen to foreigner in her house, she has big trouble! You understand? She say now I should not bring you here!" He stood up and spun out of the room.

Anna lay back, horrified. She was endless trouble for Chenxi. Below she could hear the family talking as they prepared the evening meal. The words floated up to her like an indecipherable melody, a jarring music that had no sense. A world from which she was shut out. She tried to listen to the tone of their shouting voices, but she found it impossible to know if they were angry, or happy. Were they arguing about her? Anna had never felt so alone. San Francisco and the culture she knew and understood, the place where she fitted in, where she was treated like a normal person, had never felt so far away. Reaching for her journal from her bag, Anna was struck by the ache of homesickness.

April 21st, 1989

My whole childhood I was convinced that people were the same all over the world. That all it would take for world peace and understanding was a common language. I realize now that I was wrong. Chenxi and I are nearly the same age, we have the same passion for art, but there is a gulf between us that I feel I will never be able to cross. He has had experiences in his life that in my sheltered existence I would be incapable of even imagining.

As I blunder my way through each day catching rare glimpses of who he might be, the gulf only seems to grow larger and larger, until it becomes a chasm and I stare into its blackness and wonder how deep it stretches and whether I dare jump in...

Anna put down her journal. She pulled her jacket around her, slipped on Yang Wen's slippers, and crossed the corridor to see if Chenxi was in the opposite room. She sensed she had an apology to make but she wasn't quite sure why. For being a foreigner?

The door was ajar and Anna peeked around the corner. Chenxi's cousin, Zhou Lai, was sitting at his desk doing homework. She tried to slip back out without disturbing him.

"Anna! I do my English homework. It is very hard. You help?"

"Sure," Anna said and sat on a stool near his desk. "What are you doing?"

"I practice for oral examination about 'My Family.' It very not easy."

"Difficult," Anna corrected.

"Yes, it very not difficult."

"No…oh, don't worry. What do you have to do?"

"I have talk about all family. Uncle, aunt, cousin. Because you know now in China, no more uncle, cousin, aunt. Every family must have only one children."

"Yes, I know. Let's practice then. I'll ask you a question and you answer, OK?"

"Oh, thank you. OK!"

Anna pulled her stool closer to the desk and peered down at the exercise book. "What does your father do?" she read.

"My father is teacher of science," Zhou Lai replied.

"What does your mother do?"

"My mother teacher also. She teach small school."

"My mother is *also* a teacher. She teaches at *primary* school," Anna corrected. "Your brother's school?"

"Yes, my mother is a teacher at my brother's *primary* school."

"Very good. What does your aunt do?"

"My aunt is a…how you say?" he flicked through a dictionary. "Housewife in Australia. My uncle own big Chinese restaurant and has many money," Zhou Lai boasted.

"My uncle is very rich, you say. What about your other aunt? Chenxi's mother? What does she do?"

"My aunt working in a factory."

"My aunt *works* in a factory. What about Chenxi's father? What does your uncle do?"

Zhou Lai blushed. He fiddled with his pencil then looked up. "My uncle is killed."

"My uncle is *dead*."

"No. My uncle is *killed*. In Cultural Revolution."

Anna stared at him and felt her blood run cold.

Zhou Lai looked at the door. He shook his head and lowered his voice. He drew in closer to Anna. "You know this outside China? In your country? You know this Cultural Revolution?"

"A little."

"It very no good…"

Anna didn't interrupt.

"He is killed in Cultural Revolution for love. He is marry to Chenxi mother but he love foreign woman. Older woman. His family say he very bad. They say he love foreign woman, he no love China. Chenxi only baby. Chenxi now very do not like his father. He very angry for his father love foreign woman. He no like foreigners, Chenxi. He say they trouble. That why Chenxi not polite with you…"

Anna heard the door behind her open, and Zhou Lai's eyes widened in fright. Anna's heart thudded in her chest. Without turning, she continued to read from the textbook. "What does your brother do?"

"My brother is studying at school…"

15

Mr. White stirred the sauce. On his brow pearls of sweat formed. One shook loose and rolled down through his thick gray eyebrows, along the bridge of his nose to the tip where it quivered before plopping into the red bubbles. He dabbed at his forehead with a handkerchief. Anna leaned against the kitchen doorway in a bathrobe and head towel, watching his efforts. Mr. White was making his special spaghetti sauce as a celebration for his daughter's safe arrival home, suffering no more than a slight cold. Anna picked at her nails.

"Even with the air-conditioning it gets so hot in here!" Mr. White complained.

"Dad? What was the Cultural Revolution all about?"

Mr. White lifted the wooden spoon and gingerly licked the end. Frowning, he reached for the salt and sprinkled some into the sauce. "The Cultural Revolution was Mao's last attempt to hold on to power. The Communist Party had ruled since 1949 but he'd made such a mess during the Great Leap Forward that people were beginning to doubt his capabilities. So he had to come up with something to make them believe in him again. In 1966 he cleverly manipulated the people into believing that there was a threat to the Communist revolution that could only be stopped by supporting him." Mr. White paused to pick up the spoon and taste the sauce again. "Mmm…that's better. Have you heard of the Red Guards?"

"We had a lesson on it at school, but I don't remember much. Weren't they students working for Mao? But they ended up getting out of control? Our teacher compared them a bit to the Nazi Youth."

"The Red Guards were young naïve students, your age and younger, who Mao rallied into supporting him. The education system in China has always been strict, so you can imagine, when Mao told the students that they could denounce their own teachers as enemies of the revolution, they went wild! For the students it was pure anarchy. Suddenly they had the amazing power to dress their teachers in dunce hats and parade them through the streets, the power to imprison them and beat them, and all with the support of the government."

"Wow! What were people attacked for?"

"Anything! Anything that could be twisted around into being against Mao and the Communist ideals."

"For being involved with a foreigner?"

"Especially for being involved with foreigners. Foreign companies were ransacked and looted. As were galleries and temples. Anything that was considered bourgeois and elitist and anti-Communist. Thousands of innocent people were tortured and imprisoned, killed, or driven to suicide. Families were torn apart. Students were sent to labor in the countryside and all the schools and universities were closed down. The country completely ceased to function. By the 1970s, China's economy and social order were in ruins. But Mao was such a powerful person that it wasn't until he died in 1976 that the people could gain control again. When he died, the Gang of Four—did you learn about them?"

"I can't remember who they were..."

"What *do* you learn in schools these days? They were the leaders of the Cultural Revolution and included Mao's wife. They were arrested after Mao died and the country began to return to normal. But enormous damage had been done. Can you imagine? People were left emotionally scarred. Chinese people look on that period as being the worst in recent history."

"I can understand," Anna sighed. "Imagine being denounced by your own students!"

"It wasn't only that. Everyone got into it. People were denouncing and criticizing all over the place—even in their own families!"

"Would it be possible for a wife to denounce her own husband if she suspected him of being involved with a foreigner?"

"Of course. In fact it would be very likely. People used the excuse even to settle their own personal disputes! Husbands, wives, children, parents. It was out of control. Anyway, it's good to see you're catching up on your Chinese history, dear..."

would you smell this sauce, doesn't it smell fantastic? Shall I open a bottle of wine?"

"If you like, Dad," Anna said, sitting at the table. Thoughts of Chenxi and his family whirred through her head.

Mr. White chose a bottle from the cabinet. A California red. As the wine glugged into her glass, Anna smelled the rolling hills of the Napa Valley.

April 23rd, 1989

Day by day I am piecing together information about Chenxi that helps me understand him. If I can learn about his family and his past there is a chance we could have a future. Now that I know what happened to his father I understand what he must feel about foreigners. But I'm not just a foreigner! I can be more to him than that. I want to know everything about him and he will see there is no need to be afraid…If only I could make him understand that we are meant to be together.

"Please," said Anna. "Not another week of bamboos!"

Monday morning and Anna felt excited at being in class again. Even though Chenxi hadn't turned up yet, the other students were happy to see her. Lao Li hovered protectively and Disco Ding Yue gave her furtive glances and childish grins. Anna was amazed at how quickly these faces had become familiar. She felt embarrassed that, like so many foreigners, when she'd first arrived in Shanghai, all Chinese had looked the same to her.

Her delight that she was perhaps truly becoming a member of the class turned to disappointment when Dai Laoshi approached her with another pile of newspapers. She groaned and stuck out her bottom lip like a sulky child. Dai Laoshi raised his eyebrows.

"Can't I do what they're doing?" she whined and pointed to the other students bent over their desks, painting on silk.

Dai Laoshi shrugged. He looked towards Lao Li who shrugged in turn.

Anna thumped her chest and pointed to the other students again. She mimicked them, her head down over a piece of invisible silk.

Disco Ding Yue snickered. Lao Li mumbled to Dai Laoshi who pulled at his chin. He mumbled something back in a nervous voice, and then walked to his satchel and pulled out a stack of pictures. Dai Laoshi flicked through them and brought one to Anna. The class watched in silence.

Anna looked down at the small print of a fan. Painted on the fan was a winding landscape disappearing into the mist and tiny fishermen casting a net into the rippling water.

"*Xie xie!* Thank you!" said Anna triumphantly, pleased that she had been able to make herself understood without the aid of Chenxi. She took out her ink stick and brushes.

With a little miming and coaching from Dai Laoshi, and helped by her observations of the other students during the first week, Anna deciphered the art of painting on silk. She discovered it was a matter of building up fine layers, one on top of the other, and washing the edges of the brushstrokes to blend out the lines; very different from the bold brushstrokes of Western painting. In areas where a dark color was needed, she learned to apply as many as twenty layers. White was always painted on the reverse as it was much more opaque than the black. To keep the feeling of the muted Ching dynasty colors, Dai Laoshi showed her it was enough to have the white shine through the tea-colored silk from the back.

With Chenxi not there to distract her, and unable to speak enough Chinese to chat with any of the other students, Anna soon lost herself in copying the intricate detail of the tiny mountainous landscape. Lunchtime came and went and she continued painting, engrossed in her work, declining Lao Li's offer to accompany him to the noodle shop.

At the end of the afternoon, the painting close to completion, Anna sat up and stretched, suddenly restless. The sun had shifted lower in the sky and all her classmates had long gone home. They had been impressed with her stamina and, as she pushed back from the table and looked critically at her day's work, she was pleased with what she saw.

Some of the lines were thick and shaky, but perhaps it stood up well against the replica style of the other students. Anna knew this had irritated her classmates. She didn't have to understand Chinese to be aware that they talked about her and that it unnerved them to see a foreigner so quickly learn the techniques of Chinese painting. They had all looked amused at the beginning of the day when they watched Anna lay down her first timid strokes, but were quiet when they returned from their lunch break and saw how the work was progressing.

Swirling her brushes around in the inky water, Anna contemplated how to fill the rest of the afternoon without

Chenxi. She didn't want to go home to the vacant apartment, but wandering around Shanghai in the hot crowds appealed even less.

Who else did she know in Shanghai? The French student she had smoked a joint with outside the consulate was the only person she could think of. His university was just across the river, and he had invited her. She didn't know his last name but she was sure there wouldn't be too many Laurents studying there. Feeling adventurous, she decided to pay him a visit. Even though she didn't particularly like him, he might have some decent friends. It would be good to mix with some other foreign students so that she didn't have to be so dependent on Chenxi all the time.

She took a last look at the fishermen's net shining in the foreground of her mountain landscape, then left the silk painting on her desk to dry and went in search of Laurent.

16

"Eh?" The bespectacled old man was scrunching his face behind a newspaper he hadn't taken his eyes off since Anna had approached the front desk.

"Law-*ron!*" Anna tried again, and then in faltering Chinese, "*Faguo xuesheng*. French student."

The man shook his head, his mouth turned down, and flicked over the page of his newspaper. Anna sighed.

"I know Laurent!" came a gentle voice from behind her. She turned around to see a young African man smiling at her. "He's on the third floor. I'll take you there, if you like."

"Thank you," she said, following him upstairs.

The sullen old man at reception watched over the top of his paper as the two foreigners ascended the stairs. Then he pulled out an exercise book and jotted something down.

AT THE FIRST FLOOR, the young man introduced himself as Youssou and said he was from Gabon. By the second floor Anna knew what he was studying, how many brothers and sisters he had, and his plans for the future. At Laurent's door, Youssou asked, "Is Laurent your boyfriend?"

"No, my boyfriend doesn't live on campus." She was not entirely lying, but she didn't want to give him the wrong impression.

Youssou didn't try to hide his disappointment and sighed. "Well, goodbye then?"

"Yes, I suppose." She watched Youssou walk away then knocked on the door.

Over the faint sound of jazz music came Laurent's voice, "*Shi shei?*" and when Anna didn't answer, "Who is it?"

"Er... it's Anna White... we met at the consulate..."

The door opened and the smell of incense drifted out. It took Anna a minute to recognize Laurent. He had shaved his head and was thinner than she had remembered, with dark rings around his eyes. He grinned at her.

"Hey! Come in! Come in!" he said, bowing low.

There were a couple of girls lounging in the corner on a mattress. Anna hesitated in the doorway.

"Come on!" Laurent said and tugged at her arm.

In the dim light Anna recognized one of the students who had come with Laurent to the consulate party. He was sitting at a desk rolling a joint. On an ashtray beside him balanced the stub of another joint, still smoking.

"You've come just in time," Laurent said.

Anna shook her head. "No way! That last time made me really sick!"

"I know!" Laurent groaned. "I was the one to take you home. Hey, come to think of it, you never thanked me for that!" He smirked and sidled up to Anna, pulling her down to sit on the mattress beside him.

"Actually, Chenxi was supposed to take me home," Anna lied. "I don't know why he left so early."

"He told me he has a curfew," Laurent explained.

"A curfew?"

"Where he lives. They close the gates at a certain time of night. Like they do for us here at the university. Except here, if we have to wake up the caretakers, we get away with it because we're foreigners," he said, winking. "For the Chinese it's trouble."

Anna turned this information over in her mind. Even though it sounded unjust, she felt better knowing the reason for Chenxi's strange disappearance that night. Along with the information she had gathered from her father and Zhou Lai, pieces of the Chenxi puzzle were fitting together. But she was still missing the most important piece: what did he think of her?

"Here," said the dark-haired man sitting at the desk. He handed the smoking butt down to Anna. She shook her head. He shrugged and held it out to Laurent.

"Ladies?" said Laurent, offering the joint to the two girls.

"Oh no!" they giggled and pulled themselves up, leaning on each other for support. "We're out of here, man. We're wasted!"

They stumbled to the door, laughing and swearing in a language Anna couldn't recognize, before they fell into the brightly lit corridor, slamming the door behind them.

Laurent winced. "Don't worry about them," he said. "They only come here for one thing...and it's not my body!" He chuckled at his own joke, then finished what was left of the joint before grinding it out on a small plate.

"*Je m'en vais aussi*," said the dark-haired joint-roller as he stood up. "See you, Hannah?"

"Anna."

"Yeah, whatever." He swept up the last few specks of hashish on the glass-top table and pressed them onto his tongue, then closed the door behind him.

Anna felt uneasy at being alone with Laurent in his lair but, to her relief, he now reverted to the gentlemanly manner he had used when they first met. He offered her tea and unscrewed a golden tin, from which he pinched a few scraggly leaves and dropped them into a ceramic cup with a lid. Then he picked up a large plastic thermos and told Anna he would go to the boiler room for hot water.

While he was gone, Anna studied his room. It was decorated with exquisite taste and was very different from the other students' rooms she had peered into on her way upstairs. Lengths of pale green silk patterned with dragons were tacked to the walls alongside the beds, like wallpaper. Half the floor was laid with straw matting. In the other half of the room were two desks and two cane bookshelves overloaded with Chinese books and porcelain teacups. On the floor against the walls were two mattresses made up into beds.

Laurent returned and answered her unspoken query. "My roommate is never here. He spends all his time trekking through Tibet, so I have the room to myself." He filled the two cups with hot water. "He was my roommate last year, too, and I organized to have him again this year." He smiled conspiratorially at Anna and she wondered if his roommate really existed. Laurent seemed very good at arranging things to suit his convenience.

He handed Anna a cup of tea and sat down beside her. "So what have you been doing since I saw you last?"

"I went away with Chenxi for a week. We stayed with his aunt in a town just outside of Xian."

"Really?" Laurent said, surprised.

"What's wrong with that?" Anna retorted.

"Nothing. I suppose. It's just that usually Chinese aren't allowed to have foreigners staying with them."

"It was organized by the school."

"I hope so. For Chenxi's sake."

"Who could he get into trouble with?" said Anna, but Laurent wasn't listening. "Laurent?"

Laurent put his finger to his lips.

"What?" she whispered, exasperated.

Laurent pointed to a small loudspeaker over the doorway. It crackled a little. He leaned toward her and whispered in her ear. "The intercom system. It's for calling us when we get phone calls. But it works both ways!"

"You're paranoid!" Anna giggled. "You smoke too much dope."

"Maybe," said Laurent. "But a friend of mine studying in Beijing found a bug in his bedside lamp just last week." He leaned closer until his lips brushed Anna's ear. "We're in China, my dear," he said dramatically. "Not America!"

Anna inched away and tried to think of a new subject.

The intercom gave a slight pop. "It's OK," Laurent said, his voice returning to normal. "They've finished listening." He sat back on the mattress against the wall. Anna sipped her tea.

"What do you do at your college?" Laurent asked amiably.

He was trying to make conversation to keep her in his room. She wondered why she had come. "Painting," she replied.

"Thanks. I guessed that," Laurent said. "But what kind?"

"I almost finished a copy of a Ching dynasty painting on silk today."

"Really? What's it of?"

Anna was bored. She knew he wouldn't understand. He wouldn't understand the technique, and he wouldn't understand the emotions. She was tired of trying to articulate her passion for art to people who didn't get it. Chenxi understood. He had the same passion as she did.

"A landscape. It's one of the four subject matters you can paint in Chinese painting. Landscape, Birds and Flowers, People, and Calligraphy," she droned, holding up her fingers and counting them off one by one. "Calligraphy looks the simplest but it is actually the most honored, and the most difficult. Chenxi is the only one in our class doing calligraphy."

"Is it difficult to paint on silk?"

"It's OK. Just takes getting used to I suppose. You need

special brushes. Small ones, sometimes only a hair thick, and you have to know how to choose them. Chenxi helped me choose mine."

"Really?" Laurent got up to change the CD. When he returned to the mattress, he sat closer to Anna. Their arms were touching. Anna stood to serve herself some more tea.

Between two pieces of music the room fell quiet.

"So," she asked to fill the silence, "why are you here in China?"

She tried to look interested as Laurent described his fascination with economics and his lifelong plan to outdo his father's business success by finding a trading niche with China. "It's a very delicate procedure," he explained, "to win the trust of the Chinese. By speaking Mandarin I will have an advantage over any other international interest. That's why I've been in this fucking hole for three years. It's a slow process, but it will be worth it. Marco Polo said China was a sleeping dragon, and economically that dragon is beginning to wake. It's going to be a case of first in first served and I plan to be first in. I've already made a lot of *guanxi* since I've been here."

"*Guanxi*?"

"Yeah, you know… contacts. Influence. In China everything is run by back-door politics. Like they say: It's not what you know, it's who you know. You can't get by without *guanxi* here. I plan to make a lot of money and China is the place to do it. So, in answer to your question, I guess you could say my plan is to be rich!" he finished.

"My father would love you," Anna mumbled.

"He already does, my dear. He already does!" Laurent leaned back on his elbows, smiling to himself.

"Chenxi and I are thinking of doing a painting together one day," Anna blurted out to change the subject. She didn't know where this lie came from, but once she'd started she couldn't stop herself. "Actually it's my idea and I haven't exactly discussed it with him yet, but I'm sure he'll agree. We have the same ideas in art—it's amazing. It's like, even though we don't speak the same language we understand each other through art. It's such a coincidence that we're in the same class together, you know. I mean we've grown up in such different cultures and on either side of the world, and yet, here we are: two like-minds thrown together. Like destiny or something…"

Anna stopped mid-breath. She had the awful feeling of having disclosed too much to someone she knew too little.

Laurent was inspecting his nails.

He looked up with an amused expression. "You do know Chenxi is only hanging around you for an American passport, don't you? All Chinese students want to leave China. Go abroad. Make money. There's no future for them here. You think they are interested in you? Sorry to break it to you, honey, you are just a ticket out of here. Even your precious Chenxi, my dear. They're all the same."

Anna sipped her tea. Inside her an enormous gulf opened and the tea rolled into it like a red-hot boulder. She couldn't breathe.

128

RIDING HOME THROUGH SHANGHAI in the twilight, Anna tried to make sense of her unpleasant conversation with Laurent. He seemed to know a lot about China and some of it she just couldn't believe. But what she couldn't shake from her mind was his claim about Chenxi.

Anna couldn't accept that, it was just too cruel. But hadn't her father been hinting at it since the beginning? Is that what he meant with his warning? The more she tried not to think about the possibility of being used by Chenxi, the more likely it seemed. She had always felt as if his niceness had been so obliging. Even during the week they had spent in Shendong with his family.

The clouds rumbled overhead and the air grew thick and sticky, but Anna's face was wet before the sky broke.

April 25th, 1989

Chenxi—is that all I am to you? A ticket out of China? A source of FEC? Are you only with me out of duty to the school? I feel like a fool. The worst thing, the ultimate humiliation, is that I made it so obvious that I am crazy about you. You didn't even have to make an effort to lure me; I was mesmerized from the first moment. Like a helpless insect, blindly twirling…

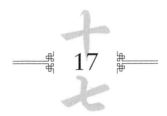

The next day it rained without stopping and Anna didn't have the heart to go in to the college. Instead she caught a taxi to and from the consulate and borrowed half a dozen American movies, sappy love stories to make her cry. She spent that day and the next in her dressing gown in the gray light of the apartment, with her feet up in front of the television. For the first time since arriving, she neglected her journal. In a rush of bitter self-pity, she considered burning the book, which had become a love letter to Chenxi. But she couldn't bring herself to do it. She tossed it into the corner of her room.

WHEN THE AIYI CAME, she sat down to watch *Casablanca* with Anna, and Anna tried to explain the storyline as best she could. The *aiyi* taught Anna a few words of Chinese and made her promise to come to eat at her house one day. After she had seen the young woman to the door, Anna realized the *aiyi* had been distracted by the movies and forgotten to do her job. Anna washed the breakfast dishes herself.

Then, at the end of her third miserable, self-pitying day, the *aiyi* brought Anna a letter from her mother. She looked at the battered envelope. The top was almost completely torn away. Her father had warned her that the mail service was unreliable but this letter had clearly been opened before it had reached her. She wondered who could possibly want to read her letters. What interest was there in the life of an eighteen-year-old girl?

She eased out the floral paper and smiled to see her mother's familiar handwriting. She considered calling her to talk about Chenxi but then reminded herself that what would start as a conversation about Anna would invariably end with her mother's own problems. She didn't feel strong enough right now to deflect her mother's loneliness. It was better this way. Anna took a deep breath.

April 17th, 1989
My dearest Anna,

I suppose you must be getting along well, as I haven't heard from you. Your sisters say you're doing fine, but it would be nice to get to talk to you myself. I rang last week when you were away and your father explained that letters take a long time to reach the States from China. I suppose that's why we haven't got a letter from you yet. You did tell me you would write often with all your news. We miss you!

Did you have a good time on your class trip? What an adventure! I don't know if I'd be up to traveling around China on my own! Where did you stay?

Are you getting along with your father? He sounded tense on the phone. Are you spending lots of time together? Father and daughter? I hope so. He told me you're enjoying your painting classes. He doesn't think much of painting, or any of the arts, really, but don't let him put you off. You know I had to give up my acting career when I married him. It's my greatest regret. I was going to be somebody. Now I'm just a leftover.

Don't forget, dear, you have a real talent in your art. I am sure that if you follow your heart and your goals, you will win your father over in the end...

That's when Anna remembered her real reason for being in China. She wasn't going to give up her art for a man and become an empty shell of regret like her mother! She put her paintbrushes in her backpack and set her alarm for early the next morning.

AS IF IN APPROVAL OF HER PLANS, the rain cleared overnight. Even though it wasn't sunny, the early morning light seemed strangely fluorescent and the streets glittered in the dawn air. Anna rode fast, imagining Chenxi on his bike, and enjoying the swishing of her tires in the wet streets as she smiled to the old people walking their birds in bamboo cages.

She overtook a street-cleaning machine and laughed at the warning music it played: "Happy Birthday." The tune cranked out like a broken car horn. When the machine slowed to round a corner, the music sounded like a record played at the wrong speed.

Anna sped through the empty market street where early-morning risers sipped on bowls of steaming tofu in broth and sleepier ones lay by their carts, huddled under plastic sheets. They rubbed their eyes, baffled, as she rode by.

At the college gate, she had the sinking feeling that she was too early. But then she spied the surly gatekeeper arriving with a rinsed tin bowl in his hand. He glared at Anna as he opened the gate. She nodded her thanks and wheeled her bike into the quiet grounds.

Two steps at a time, Anna ran up the stairwell and opened the classroom door. She was determined to finish her work on silk. The last thing she expected when she reached her desk was that the landscape painting would be gone.

Alone in the classroom Anna roared in indignant rage, sweeping papers off the desks around her. Her discovery was the culmination of a lamentable week and now she blamed Chenxi for everything. She blamed him for coveting and stealing her work, and she blamed him for her personal unhappiness. When she had finished blaming him for all her misery, she tidied the papers back onto the desks and took out a fresh piece of silk to start again.

This time her first brushstrokes were deft and accurate. Her lines were strong and dense where they should be and then round and expressive in other places. The colors mixed well and blended into each other without a trace. She painted furiously.

One by one her classmates trickled in. Curious, they circled Anna and stood over her desk, breathing heavily, watching the mountains and misty valleys of Anna's miniature landscape come to life. Then they too settled at their desks and began to work. Dai Laoshi wandered in halfway through the morning and did the rounds of the classroom. Satisfied that all his students were hard at work, he left to drink tea and smoke cigarettes with the other teachers. Chenxi didn't turn up. Anna was relieved because she hadn't worked out what to say to him yet.

She was finishing the ragged mountain peaks when, as if automated by an interior clock, the students pushed back from their desks. Laughing and shouting, they rushed off for lunch. Lao Li lingered. Anna looked up at him and smiled. "Shall we go and get some lunch?"

Lao Li stared at her.

She mimed a bowl near her mouth and shoveled in imaginary food. Lao Li laughed and said, "*Hao! Hao!*" She'd been here long enough now to know he meant "Good!"

LAURENT WAS AT THE NOODLE SHOP. He had just finished eating and was lighting a cigarette at one of the tables outside in the sun. He smiled at Anna and beckoned her over. She noticed how the soup had left a greasy smear on his chin. He wiped it off on the back of his hand and Anna wondered if she had been staring. She had allowed herself to stare while living in China. She would have to drop the habit when she got back home.

"How are you?" He spoke to Anna, but looked over her shoulder at Lao Li.

"This is Lao Li," Anna said.

Laurent said a few words to Lao Li in Chinese and, much to Anna's annoyance, Lao Li pulled up a stool beside Laurent and the two men proceeded to chat like old friends.

Anna also sat and held up one finger to the manager of the stall, the way she had asked for a bowl of noodle soup in the past. But Laurent laughed and ordered for her in Chinese. Although she hated his smugness, she hated her own inability to speak Chinese even more.

"So, Lao Li tells me he's a classmate of yours," Laurent said, as the bowls were set in front of them. He had ordered another bowl for himself to keep Anna and Lao Li company and now he twisted his chopsticks expertly into the mass, slurping the noodles up to his lips. Lao Li drank broth from the bowl.

"Mmm," Anna answered, not looking up. The soup burned her mouth. She tried to look as though she were concentrating on her chopsticks.

"I just asked him about Chenxi, you know, to find out about him for you," Laurent added, looking over his bowl at Anna for her reaction.

"Laurent!" Anna spluttered. She glanced at Lao Li to see

if he had understood. Lao Li was shoveling noodles into his mouth. His glasses had fogged up with steam.

"Lao Li tells me Chenxi is always in trouble. He says it's in his blood—his father was the same. Except his father was killed for it. Everybody knows."

"Shut up!" Anna looked across at Lao Li, but she was desperate to hear more.

Laurent took his time finishing his mouthful.

He swallowed and continued. "Lao Li says Chenxi's in everybody's bad books. He's a stirrer. One false move and the authorities will jump. Good reason for him to try to get a visa out of the country, isn't it?" Laurent laughed.

"I'm going back to class," Anna said, standing up. She left her bowl of noodles unfinished. She had heard enough.

"No, seriously," Laurent said, grabbing her by the arm. "I might be wrong about the visa bit; maybe he does only want to be your friend. But the way Lao Li talks, Chenxi already causes enough trouble for himself. Stay away from him. You don't need to make it worse. They will look for any excuse..."

"They, they, they!" Anna shouted, pushing his arm away. "Stay out of my fucking business! You know what you are, Laurent? You're just a fucking paranoid drug addict!"

Laurent blanched. As Anna spun around, she noticed that all the people in the shop had fallen quiet and were staring at her. She hadn't even begun to walk away before she regretted what she had said. She stomped on through the marketplace, shoving past the staring peasants. "What's his problem?" she fumed. "Why is he so suspicious of everyone? Has living in China made him so cynical?"

Her steps echoed in the empty corridor as she stormed up through the college building. She reached the second floor out of breath and paused at the door of the classroom. Somebody was already in there. She peered through the dirty glass. Chenxi was sitting on a desk staring at his painting pinned to the wall, the painting she had helped him complete. Anna could only see his back, but his shoulders were hunched. He got up and walked to her desk and looked at her painting on silk. He picked it up and held it close to his face, examining it before laying it flat again.

Deep down Anna had known all along that it wasn't Chenxi who had taken her work. It could have been any of the college students who filtered in and out of the unlocked classroom. Looking at him through the classroom window, so diminished in front of the masterpiece he had created, she was filled with a familiar falling sensation. She watched him stare at his work. She watched him reverently unpin it from the wall and roll it tight. She watched him slip it under his desk. What anguish was he hiding from her behind his habitual blank expression? As if he felt her thoughts, Chenxi turned around. Seeing Anna's face at the window, he composed himself.

Anna walked into the room and perched on the edge of her desk. "I had to do a new painting," she said. "Someone stole my other one."

"I heard," Chenxi said, smiling. "You get too good."

Anna blushed. She pointed to Chenxi's painting under his desk. "Why don't you show the work to anyone here?"

Chenxi shrugged and looked away. "You do not understand," he mumbled.

"How can I understand anything if you never explain anything to me?" she blurted. "Why do you always treat me like a stupid foreigner? I've been in China nearly four weeks now. I am leaving in just a few days. I have spent so much time with you. And it seems every day I spend with you, the less I know you! I want to understand! What are you afraid of? What are you trying to protect me from?"

Anna bit her lip. All she could hope now was that the little crack she had opened wouldn't close again. She turned away.

Chenxi was watching Anna.

"I'm sorry," Anna whispered. "It's none of my business, I know."

A smile flickered at the corner of Chenxi's lips. "I take you somewhere, now," he said. "Then you understand."

"What did you say?"

"Come with me," said Chenxi, holding out his hand. "You see there is one person he understand my art!"

18

The sunlight cut the worn parquet floor into geometric shapes. The air was thick with cigarette smoke, and ceramic teacups littered the floor. Some of them contained the dried black remains of tea leaves, others the crystalized splinters of evaporated rice wine. In the darkest corner a bearded man lay smoking in a bed.

Outside his door two voices murmured. The man rose and slid his feet into a pair of threadbare slippers. He shuffled to a chair over which his shirt lay and checked his watch before answering the door.

"We cannot come see him before two o'clock," Chenxi whispered to Anna in front of the peeling wooden door. They were standing in a leafy courtyard where the sound of the traffic could be heard only as a distant hum. "He likes sleep until late."

It had taken them the best part of an hour to reach this spot. It was on the outskirts of Shanghai and they had caught two buses. On the way Anna tried to find out where they were going, but Chenxi remained as secretive as ever. The mystery only grew now that she found herself in front of an ancient Chinese building, listening to him speak in a hushed tone, as if they were in an art gallery or a church.

The door creaked open and a slight Chinese man with a wispy white beard and dark rings under the slits of his eyes peered out at them. His face lit up when he saw Chenxi but he frowned when he saw Anna. He slapped Chenxi on the back, squeezed his shoulder, and accepted with grace the plastic container of pork dumplings Chenxi had bought for him on the way. He opened the door wide and gestured for them to come in. All the while his gaze remained fixed upon Anna.

Anna smiled meekly and stepped over a worn doorjamb into the room. As Chenxi made to follow her, the bearded man grabbed him by the shoulder and pulled him back into the courtyard. She heard them talking outside. She recognized one term that had become too familiar to her since her arrival in China: *wai guo ren*.

As her eyes adjusted to the darkness, Anna looked around. A rumpled four-poster bed took up one corner, and a carved rosewood table another. She stepped forward and tripped over a little ceramic cup. The room smelled of cigarette smoke, sweat, and sickly sweet rice wine. Lowering herself onto a three-legged stool, Anna peered at the hand-painted posters on the walls. She stared at the slashing red Chinese characters as if by willpower she could make herself understand them. They remained as indecipherable as hieroglyphics.

Chenxi stepped into the room followed by the bearded man. They squatted on stools and began to talk as if Anna weren't there. Soon another young Chinese man poked his head through the doorway. Chenxi laughed and pulled up a stool. The man with the white beard got up to fetch a bottle of rice wine. The newcomer caught sight of Anna and his mouth dropped open. He looked at Chenxi, who mumbled something in Chinese, and then nodded respectfully toward Anna. Turning back to Chenxi, he pulled out a pack of cigarettes. The three of them, all talking in loud, excited voices, played a game of offering, refusing, and exchanging cigarettes. Anna had seen it before. It seemed there was status attached to who could offer the most expensive cigarettes and how generously they could be forced upon the other men.

After this ritual they all sat down again and lit their cigarettes in silence. The tall young newcomer turned to Anna and held out his pack of cigarettes. Anna shook her head and smiled politely. She had heard that the only women who smoked in China were artists or prostitutes, so she hoped Chenxi had introduced her as the former.

Suddenly the newcomer slapped his thigh and pulled a book of photographs from his top pocket. He handed them shyly to the bearded man without a word, and Chenxi drew in closer to peer over his shoulder. Even though for her they were upside-down, Anna could see from where she was sitting that they were photos of paintings. The bearded man squinted at them, flicking through the book. He stopped at a gray painting of a gray body of a man floating on his back in a pool of gray water. A single red peony, like a bloodstain, bloomed over his chest.

Anna looked over at the tall young man's face. It was tense with expectation.

"*Bu zuo, bu zuo,*" the bearded man murmured, nodding his head. The young man, relieved, broke into a rapid monologue. The bearded man didn't speak again.

"*Ni hao! Ni hao!*" Three more young men appeared in the doorway and Chenxi stood to let them in. One of them, with hair down to his waist, carried a battered art portfolio. Another, with a shaven head, had a roll of paper under his arm. They jumbled into the room and the cigarette game started again.

The afternoon dragged by. Anna sat in her corner, sipping tea, and observed young artists coming and going, making their pilgrimage to this strange, quiet, bearded man. He spoke only a few words about each painting or drawing presented to him, but each time he did the noisy artists fell silent, hanging off his every word.

If the bearded man was preoccupied, the artists took their work to Chenxi, who discussed it with them at length, his face serious and his voice passionate and animated. Chenxi's pockets became so crammed with the foreign cigarettes offered to him that he had to start putting them into his bag and behind his ears.

Anna felt bored and irritated. The room was unbearably smoky and the noise of the young artists' excited chatter was annoying. She had no idea how much time had passed but, judging by the changing light and the cramp in her legs, she guessed it was not far off evening. She stood up and stretched.

The young men stopped their conversations and stared as if she had just appeared out of nowhere. Anna blushed.

Chenxi walked over to her. "What's wrong?" he said.

"I want to go home!" She knew she sounded like a sulky child, but she didn't care.

Chenxi sighed. He walked back to the young man whose work he had been looking at and said a few words. The young man nodded. Then Chenxi went to the man with the wispy white beard and took both his hands in his. The bearded man squeezed Chenxi's shoulder and nodded without smiling. The room went quiet.

"OK," Chenxi said. He turned to Anna and held the front door open for her. She stepped out into the brightness, to find the sun much lower in the sky.

"Who is that man?" Anna demanded as they made their way out of the courtyard to the bus stop. "Does he think he's some kind of guru or something? I don't like him!"

Chenxi glared at her. "It do not matter if you do not like him. He is very important man. For me, he is most important man in all of China!"

"So, who is he?" Anna repeated.

"Old Wolf, we call him," Chenxi smiled to himself. "He is heart of art in China. Without him, there is no true artists. He is our freedom."

Anna frowned. She was tired of Chenxi's cryptic replies. It was too difficult to understand anything in China. Was it only the language barrier or something more? She felt so tired of it all.

Anyway, she consoled herself, she had only one week left and she would be back in the States. Back in her clean, quiet city where life was so simple and her friends' biggest worries were deciding which pair of jeans to put on that day.

She was tired of the noise, tired of the pollution. Tired of being stared at and pointed at and jostled. Tired of being the foreigner. But most of all she was tired of trying to understand Chenxi. It had been foolish to expect that she could.

She looked at him now as they heaved themselves onto the crowded bus and felt inexplicably annoyed with him.

They stood pressed against each other in the lurching bus without speaking. Before, Anna would have reveled in Chenxi's proximity. Now she just felt hot and bad-tempered. The odor of sweaty bodies was making her nauseous. Chinese people even smelled different.

At their stop, Chenxi and Anna forced their way off the bus, as another bus pulled in at the stop opposite.

"Come on!" shouted Chenxi. "Quick. That our bus!" He dashed across the road, dodging the surge of cyclists, and clambered onto the bus. "Come on!" he shouted again to Anna, who stood hesitant on the other side of the road. Between them, the cyclists were an unyielding mass. Chenxi hung out of the doorway by one hand. "Come on!"

Anna took two steps off the curb, but stepped back quickly as a cyclist swerved past. She looked up again and the bus groaned out into the street. With Chenxi still on it.

"The bastard!" Anna cursed. She felt angry tears prickling in her eyes. "He really doesn't give a shit about me!" She stood trembling on the pavement watching the bus slide into the traffic. Her stomach heaved in panic. "I don't know where I am! I don't even know how to ask the way home!" She was totally dependent on Chenxi, and she hated him all the more for it.

Tears flowing down her cheeks, she pushed her way through the crowd in the direction the bus had taken. Around her loomed faces with staring black eyes. In her head echoed the chant "*Wai guo ren! Wai guo ren!* Foreigner! Foreigner!"

Terrified, she pushed blindly on, trying to run. Sweat and tears stung her eyes. She crossed a road and then another. Nothing looked familiar. The bus had disappeared.

She reached a spot where the crowd was seething, almost impenetrable. Anna squeezed her eyes tight and lunged with all her might.

She broke through into the middle of a circle and opened her eyes to look at what the crowd had gathered to see.

Crouched on the pavement was Chenxi. He lifted his face to her. She saw the blood and screamed.

19

In the taxi, Anna held Chenxi's head in her arms. She could feel his blood seeping into her shirt. The driver rested his hand on the horn, inching his way through the traffic. She looked down at Chenxi. His eyes were shut.

"Chenxi?" she whispered.

"Mmm?"

"Are you sure you don't want to go to hospital? You might have a concussion."

Chenxi lifted his head and scowled in pain. "No!" he said. "I tell you. No hospital!"

Anna stared out the window. Looking at his bleeding face turned her stomach. A cyclist bumped off the front of the taxi and glared in at them. The meter ticked.

At the entrance to her apartment block, she paid the driver and dragged Chenxi out of the taxi. He leaned his whole weight into her. The sentry stared at them as she and Chenxi limped past, then he shuffled back into his box and picked up the phone. In the elevator Chenxi seemed to wake up a bit. He opened his eyes wide in panic. "I cannot come here. What if your father here?"

"So what!" scoffed Anna, but she was thankful to see a note in her father's handwriting on the dining room table.

Anna led Chenxi into the bathroom and sat him on the closed toilet seat. She took out cotton wool and filled a cup with warm water. Breathing deeply, she turned toward Chenxi's battered face and set to work. Tenderly, she cleared away the dried blood around his nose and mouth. Working up to his forehead she discovered the source of most of the blood. Chenxi winced as Anna dabbed at the open wound.

Anna grimaced in sympathy, and every now and then she had to stop and take another big breath before going on. Soon Chenxi's face was clean. Anna fastened a big wad of white gauze to his forehead. She shuddered. Chenxi opened his eyes.

"It's finished," she whispered.

Chenxi gave her a smile. His left eye was nearly closed.

Anna took Chenxi's hands in her own and pleaded, "Please Chenxi, now will you tell me what happened?"

His face clouded over and he looked away.

"Chenxi?"

He sighed. "I try get off bus for get you. The ticket man... how you say?"

"Conductor."

"Conductor close bus door and not let me out. I shout at

147

him and tell him to let me off bus. Then he shout at me that I must buy ticket. I say I do not want buy ticket. I am want get off bus. He tell me he know who I am. He say he know I am artist. He say I am trouble." Chenxi's voice lowered. "He say he know I am friends with foreign devil. Then he open door of bus and shout: 'You want get off? You get off! I not want you on my bus!' And he push me onto road and bus still move. Many people on bikes hit into me. One man help me onto footpath. People standing all around me shouting, shouting. Then you come."

Anna gasped. "But you have to tell the police! You can't let them do that to you!"

Chenxi flinched. "If I tell police it is worse. I have one friend report to police and they beat him. They beat him with sticks with electricity. He is in hospital for long time after that. The police do not like us. They do not like artists. They think we corrupt good Chinese society. You remember Old Wolf we saw today? The police would like find him. They say he bad element. They know I in Old Wolf group, but they cannot do anything to me, I do not do anything wrong. They would like very much to catch me do something wrong." He paused. "They do not like that I with foreign girl, but they cannot do anything because it is you father ask for me."

"But Chenxi, this is insane! There must be something you can do! This goes against basic human rights. There are people who can protect you…"

"In America, maybe," Chenxi said bitterly. "In China if you choose to be a true artist like me, not artist for the government like everyone in the college, if you choose to be free, you are on your own."

"I have to do something to help," Anna whispered. "I have to do something." She felt a sob rising and looked away.

Chenxi lifted her chin. "You already help me," he said with a soft smile.

Anna wailed, "But what? What have I done since I've been here except make trouble for you? As if you didn't have enough trouble of your own! Tell me, what? What have I done?"

"You have give me courage to follow my heart. Before you came I not sure if I really can be artist, I think maybe is too dangerous." He was staring at a spot over Anna's shoulder. He turned then to look at her. "You have teach me what is to be free."

Inside Anna a thousand voices roared, but she obeyed only one of them. Before she knew it, she had taken Chenxi's battered face and pressed her mouth to his. When she drew back, his eyes were wide with surprise.

As if waking from a trance, Chenxi stood up. "I must go!" he said. "You father home soon. At my home too my mother wait!"

And he was gone.

20

Anna drifted out of the brightly lit bathroom to find the living room in purple darkness. She peered out the window just in time to catch a glimpse of Chenxi running down the street. She groaned to herself, "What have I done?"

At the gate, Mr. White's dark car drew to a halt. Two people got out. Anna's father and… she couldn't identify the second person in the dark. She rushed to turn the lights on and clear up the bathroom.

"Look who I met at the consulate!" Anna's father called as he opened the apartment door. Laurent slunk in behind him. "I thought you'd be happy to see each other again!" Mr. White was in high spirits. A little drunk, Anna guessed.

Laurent walked toward Anna and tried to kiss her on both cheeks. Anna cringed. "*Bonsoir*, Anna," he said.

Mr. White wandered off into the kitchen. "I invited Laurent back for a bite to eat. The *aiyi* usually leaves something in the fridge on Fridays… let's see. Yes, here we are… fried noodles. How does that sound? I just have to heat it up in the microwave. Will you set the table, dear?"

Laurent raised his eyebrows at Anna.

"With pleasure," Anna sneered, glaring back at Laurent.

Anna set out the bowls on the table while Laurent watched her. Mr. White appeared with the noodles. He placed them on the table and put on some classical music.

"Sit down, Laurent. Sit down."

Anna sat on the other side of her father. She stared down into her bowl.

"Laurent tells me he's planning on opening a Sino-Franco business franchise here when he's finished his studies, Anna." Mr. White was clearly impressed. "He has only one more year of studying Chinese and he'll be ready to start."

Anna helped herself to the noodles. Laurent, realizing nobody was going to serve him, took some noodles for himself. Mr. White seemed to have forgotten his food. "I like a man who knows where he's going," he said, winking at Laurent.

Laurent smiled back.

"Anyway, Anna, that got me thinking. I was discussing your future with Laurent and I decided that perhaps it wouldn't be a bad thing to follow in his footsteps. Mandarin is a very useful language for business, these days. So, this is what I have to propose…" He paused for emphasis. Laurent looked into his noodles. "How about you staying on and studying at the university with Laurent?"

Mr. White leaned back, satisfied. Laurent shot Anna a furtive glance.

"Dad!"

"You wouldn't have to worry about the money, dear. I'll cover that. And you could stay on the campus with all the other foreign students. That would be fun, wouldn't it?"

"Dad!"

"Really, I think it's an excellent idea. And it would give you both a good opportunity to get to know each other." He winked at Laurent again. Laurent looked away.

Anna pushed her chair back from the table. "Can we talk about this another time, Dad?" she said. "I really don't think this is something we should be discussing right now." She shook her head at Laurent.

As Anna left the room, she heard her father whispering to Laurent, "Really! It's impossible to get an answer out of that girl!"

She sat on her bed, trembling with fury. Once again she realized how much her father had always made all the decisions for everyone in her family. Even though he no longer lived with Anna and her sisters, her mother still deferred to him when an important decision had to be made. Worse, Anna knew she was at fault herself. Following the path her father paved for her had always been the easiest route, and she willingly chose it. Why couldn't she stand up to him? Why couldn't she insist on doing what she wanted to do? Was it because, if she did defy him, she would have to make all those decisions by herself?

The following morning was Saturday, and Mr. White was up early to get in half a day's work. Like every Saturday, he would be back in time for a late lunch with Anna. Grateful to have the morning to herself, she rolled over to her bedside table and picked up her journal. Confusion whirred through her head. If she could just get it down on paper she might be able to order her thoughts a little.

April 30th, 1989
Chenxi—I can still feel your kiss but when I think of you it is as if I am floating in a void. Darkness surrounds me and all I see in front of me is your bleeding face. And those eyes that I find so hard to read. I have never known eyes so hard to read before...

Anna wrote into the morning. Everything that drifted through her head was transferred onto paper. As the words formed in front of her eyes, page after page, she emptied herself. In writing she could pretend her life was fiction. One great novel whose ending was out of her hands.

She put down her pen only when she heard the *aiyi* unlock the front door. She stood up and stretched. Not in the mood to converse in their bumbling, improvised sign language, Anna put her journal back on the bedside table and pulled on her clothes.

When she heard the *aiyi* washing up in the kitchen, she slipped out, for a walk through Fuxing Park.

The fashion for schoolchildren in Shanghai that year was

yo-yos. A group of ten-year-olds with red faces and red scarves stood in a circle, their hair sweaty on their foreheads, practicing their tricks. These were fat children, under-exercised and overfed, spoiled boys with no siblings to attract attention away from them in a family of doting parents, grandparents, uncles, and aunts. One stopped his yo-yo in mid-swing and grunted to his friend, "*Wai guo ren!*" His friend looked up.

As Anna approached, the boys drew into a line and began a low earnest chant: "*Wai guo ren. Wai guo ren. Wai guo ren.*"

Encouraged by Anna's frown, and with the excitement that comes from being in a group, the boys called louder: "*Wai guo ren! Wai guo ren!*"

Anna passed, and the boys closed in behind her. Ten-year-old boys who like to pull the legs off crickets for fun, ten-year-olds with nasty laughs. Behind her, the chant grew louder: "*Wai guo ren! Wai guo ren! Wai guo ren!*"

She walked faster, pretending not to hear.

Leaving the park and the boys behind, she walked down a street she hadn't taken before. It was a side street and quiet compared to the roar of Huai Hai Lu. She stopped at a shop on the corner and a procession of curious onlookers gathered and pushed from behind to see what she would buy. The shopkeeper was embarrassed and got up reluctantly from his stool in front of the television. He called his wife out for a look. Anna tried the little Chinese the *aiyi* had taught her.

"*Wo yao mai…*" she began, but she didn't know the word for grapes, so she pointed to a small green bunch hanging in front of her. The crowd behind her howled with laughter.

"*Wo yao mai…wo yao mai…*" they mimicked. "She wants to buy grapes!" they shouted at the passersby who hadn't stopped yet. "The foreigner's going to buy grapes!"

The shopkeeper thrust the grapes at her, and Anna held out her purse for him to take out the money. A toothless old woman, shoving among the crowd at Anna's elbow, pushed the shopkeeper's hand away and took some coins from Anna's purse to give him. He grumbled to the old woman but she snapped back and prodded at the sign beneath the grapes with a brown fingernail.

"Thank you," Anna said, smiling at the old woman. She popped a grape into her mouth. The woman's eyes flashed and she shrieked at Anna, shaking her head and her hands. Anna spat the grape out. The woman pulled the bunch from Anna's grasp and plucked a single grape. Methodically she peeled the skin with her stained fingertips, pushing the shiny bald fruit toward Anna's mouth when she had finished. The crowd behind her was still tutting at Anna and shaking their fingers at the unpeeled grapes.

Anna ate what was left of the grape, thanked the old woman again, and tucked the rest of the bunch into her bag. She turned to walk away but the crowd was thick around her. They shifted a little to let her push past.

ANNA ARRIVED BACK AT THE APARTMENT to find her father sitting at the table, reading. The dishes from breakfast lay all around him.

"Hi," he said coolly, peering over the top of his glasses. "Where have you been?" He pulled out a chair for Anna.

"Didn't the *aiyi* finish cleaning today?" Anna said, stacking the dishes. She took them to the kitchen and ran water into the sink. Her father came in behind her.

"I sacked her," he said.

"Oh? I must admit I didn't find her that conscientious."

"I caught her looking through my papers. I've suspected her for a while. The consulate's lining me up with a replacement next week."

"Why would she want to be looking at engineering contracts?" Anna joked. She turned off the water and reached down into the bottom cupboard for a pair of rubber gloves.

"I have some very important documents here," he said, offended. "There may be many other companies interested in seeing them."

"Sorry, Dad," Anna said. She remembered Laurent, convinced that he was being spied on, and wondered if living in Shanghai encouraged paranoia.

Still, she was glad the *aiyi* seemed to have preoccupied her father for the time being. She didn't feel in the mood for any more lectures about her future.

Anna took three pieces of white bread and some cheese on a plate and slipped out of the kitchen to her room. Without the *aiyi*, there was no chance of her father organizing a meal.

IN THEIR SMALL ROOM, Chenxi waited for his mother to return, with a live fish or a bag of dumplings in her basket for them to share. Before him, on the table where they ate and worked, lay the painting he had been working on. He squinted. It was getting dark and he stood up to turn on the lamp. The painting was finished. And Chenxi was pleased with it. He would give it to Anna when he saw her next.

21

"**I** have something for you," Chenxi whispered to Anna as he passed her desk. Anna looked up at him in surprise. She had been concentrating so hard on her painting that she hadn't noticed him come in. It was Monday morning. Anna had been worried about him all weekend. Apart from a dark ring around his left eye, Chenxi's face had almost healed, but he had worn his hair down to cover the neat bandage on his forehead. Anna felt a rush of tenderness toward him.

"I meet you at your apartment after class," he said.

Anna nodded.

The morning was tedious. Anna glanced at Chenxi several times, hoping for a secret look, but as usual, and as if nothing had ever happened between them, he spoke to her only to translate something important the teacher said.

At one stage, Lao Li caught Anna gazing at Chenxi. He stared at her. Anna put her head down again and tried to concentrate on her painting. She was working on another copy of a fan on silk, this time a bird and flower composition, but somehow it lacked the interior force of the landscape she had painted on her own the day after she got her mother's letter.

They ate noodles together at lunchtime with Lao Li, as they always did. When Chenxi's leg brushed against Anna's under the table, she looked at him to see if it was a sign, but his head was bowed over his bowl of noodles.

For the afternoon class they again had a model. This time it was an old man in a loincloth. No matter how Anna worked, she couldn't seem to capture his sagging face. Normally this task would have been easy for her but having Chenxi in the room was too distracting.

Finally it was time to return home. Anna sauntered out in front of Chenxi, while he packed up his brushes. She met him at the bike shelter. Even as he unlocked his bike he only glanced at Anna, waving and calling to students all around him as they wobbled off home.

Anna followed Chenxi as he rode out the front gate. For an instant, she held her breath and waited to see if he would turn left in the direction of her apartment, or right, the direction of his own home. The secret message whispered to her that morning seemed now merely a dream. He turned left, and she sped to catch up.

Chenxi rode fast, as always. Anna concentrated all her efforts on keeping up with him, never quite reaching his side. It was only as they passed the music conservatory and rounded the corner onto her cul-de-sac that Chenxi slowed, allowing Anna, breathless and sweaty, to draw level with him.

She wheeled her bike next to Chenxi as they passed through the high black gate of the apartment block. The sentry's hawk-eye was fixed upon them.

"HERE," SAID CHENXI when they were seated on her father's ivory silk couch. "Something of me to take home with you to America." From his shabby backpack, he drew out a roll of newspaper and handed it to Anna. She pulled her legs up underneath her and crossed them ceremoniously before unrolling the paper.

Inside, delicately painted on a long piece of silk, sat a woman on a golden throne, hands resting in her lap. Her emerald and sapphire robe fell in luxurious folds over her knees and into the landscape, the fabric itself patterned with mountainous peaks, spiraling clouds, and valleys, until it was impossible to decipher where the woman's body ended and where the landscape began. She wore an ornamental headdress, like that of a Chinese empress. But the hair that escaped from beneath it was fair and curling instead of shiny black.

When Anna looked at the tiny face under the white powder and red painted lips, she recognized it. She saw herself reflected in the brilliant blue eyes and knew the face was her own.

She rolled the painting back into its newspaper shell and stood up to place it on the coffee table. She turned back to Chenxi, then kneeled on the carpet in front of him and looked up into his eyes. She kissed them, those expressionless eyes that had troubled her for so long. Chenxi did not move. Anna kissed the bridge of his nose, and waited. She began to tremble. Closing her eyes she brought her mouth close to his, not quite touching. There she waited, breathing the same air, until Chenxi kissed her.

He tasted warm and sour and smelled like cinnamon and the feel of his skin was softer than she could have imagined and so different from anything she had known. He seemed to be waiting for her lead, so she took his palm and placed it against her ribs, underneath her shirt. There it slid upward and she shivered as he explored her breasts and wondered how different she felt to him. He drew back and played curiously with one of her long curls, and she, in turn, ran her hands through his long black hair, surprised at how coarse it was after the softness of his skin.

Anna knew they had reached a point where, at home in San Francisco, a bumbling conversation about contraception might begin; but not wanting to spoil the moment she silently counted the days since her last period and decided it was worth the risk. She had taken risks before. Chenxi flinched as she reached for his belt buckle and she wondered if Chinese girls were so brazen, but then they were kissing again and it was so easy to slide out of their clothes. His body was long and sleek, smooth and hairless. Just as she had imagined it would be.

He seemed to like that she was taking charge and they were both breathing heavily by now. Her head began to spin. She pulled him down on top of her and he kissed her neck and then the space between her breasts. She slid her hands along his ribs to the curve of his lower back, then shuddered when he slid inside her and arched her back to meet him.

She had fantasized about this moment for so long and now that he was between her thighs he felt like a stranger again. He moved urgently, but seemed distant. His eyes were closed. His breathing quickened and through the fog of her desire she thought of asking him to pull out, just to be safe, but then it was over. It was too fast. Anna tried not to feel disappointed. Was it always this way for girls?

He rolled off and they both lay on the carpet, staring up at the ceiling. The air around them simmered with awkwardness and desire. Anna propped herself up to look into Chenxi's face. The skin on his face was smooth and tight. The muscles around his eyes hardly moved, even when he smiled. But when she looked deeper, even deeper, Anna glimpsed a slow fire roaring. Then it was gone.

"I must leave!" His voice was hoarse, and before she could protest, he was dressing.

"Stay!"

"Don't ask me to."

"Then walk with me in the park." She couldn't be parted from him yet.

In the entrance to Fuxing Park squatted the old fortune-teller. Anna had often watched him reading people's hands, as

162

she read their faces, trying to determine whether they were happy with the outcome. Sometimes he had spotted her spying and called, "Tell your fortune? Tell your fortune, Little Miss Foreigner? I speak very good English. I tell you who you marry!" But Anna had always been too shy.

Today, with Chenxi by her side and the sensation of his skin still burning in hers, she felt daring and pulled him over to the stall. The fortune-teller's face lit up.

"Come on!" Anna pleaded coquettishly, but Chenxi stuck his hands in his pockets. "Just for fun!"

"I no believe that rubbish!"

"Oh come on!" Anna giggled and thrust her palm into the old man's weathered ones. The fortune-teller's brow wrinkled as he traced the lines along Anna's palm with a yellow nail.

"You have long life..." he murmured. "You have lots of money and success..." Anna smiled to herself. It was always the same.

The old man's eyebrows shot up. "You have many children!" he squealed. "With him!" He pointed to Chenxi. Anna pulled her hand away as if it had been burned.

"Oh nonsense!" She laughed.

"It's true! It's true. You will marry this man!"

"Come on!" Chenxi snapped. "Let's go." He fished a coin out of his pocket to give the fortune-teller, but the old man grabbed hold of Chenxi's palm.

The fortune-teller's eyes widened in horror. "And you, my son," he crowed, "will follow the path of your father!"

Chenxi pulled Anna by the arm into the park, while the

163

fortune-teller cackled behind them.

"Don't worry," Anna said. "I don't believe in that crap either. It's just for fun. They say the same to everyone."

"We each choose our own road to walk down," Chenxi muttered, staring ahead. Anna skipped to catch up with him.

IN THE SHELTER OF AN ORNATE ROCK DISPLAY, Chenxi and Anna found a bench hidden from curious eyes. At their feet a goldfish pond writhed with shiny scales that thrashed to the surface when Chenxi cleared his throat and spat into the water. Anna stared at the huge goggle eyes of the goldfish and wondered how to begin.

"Chenxi, I've thought about this for a long time." Her heart was pounding. She was about to declare her true feelings for him, and she couldn't bear to think they might be rejected. But if she didn't speak now, she would never know. After today, she was sure it was impossible that he couldn't love her, too.

"I think there's a way I can help you," she began.

Chenxi lit a cigarette.

Anna took a deep breath. "I can bring you back to San Francisco with me. There you will be safe. We would have to get married for the papers, of course, but the most important thing is you will leave China."

Chenxi studied the top of his cigarette and blew on it. "I do not want leave China. Why you think I want to leave China?"

"Oh Chenxi! You're just cut up about what that old man said.

164

He freaked you out, that's all. Chenxi, I know what happened to your father. I know how you feel about foreigners, but you're just being ridiculous! I am offering for you to come to America with me. To leave China. You're not safe here. In America you will be safe."

"I do not want leave China."

"You don't want to leave China?" Anna was incredulous. "But all students want to leave China!" Anna stumbled. She hadn't expected this!

"But, you see, Anna, I am not 'all students.'" His smile was forced.

Anna stared at him. Then she turned and glared at the fish pond. "You're crazy!" She was hurt and she wanted to hurt him. "You stay here and you're finished!"

"Yes," said Chenxi, grinning now. "I am crazy. That what my mother say, that what my college say, that what Chinese government say…" His grin turned into a sneer. "They all say, like you, to be artist is crazy. If that what you think, then I am crazy. What you want I do in America? Open restaurant, like all Chinese who go to America?"

"You can be an artist, Chenxi! You can be free!"

"There is no use for me to be artist in America. There I have nothing to say. I am artist for China. China is my country that I hate and that I love, but China is me. In the U.S. of A. I am nothing. In the U.S. of A. it mean nothing to be free!" Chenxi ground his butt out with his foot. He brought his face close to Anna's. "You see,'" he whispered, "not all Chinese want to go to you precious America!"

165

Then he stood up and was gone.

THE SCHOOLCHILDREN PACKED UP their yo-yos and left. The strolling couples gathered beneath the trees and Fuxing Park became mauve and mysterious. In perfect synchrony, the lamps flickered, then gleamed. Under one of them spun a dizzy moth, under another sat Anna. When her legs began to numb and her bare arms to prickle in the evening chill, she stood up, crossed the park, and walked home.

The next day when Anna turned up at the college to find Chenxi wasn't there, she was relieved. The second day, annoyed. The third day, she began to worry. When she was eating noodles with Lao Li, she blurted out, "Lao Li, Chenxi *zai nar*? Where is Chenxi?"

Lao Li pushed away his bowl, grinning mysteriously, and beckoned for Anna to follow him. They wheeled their bikes into the crowded street and rode side by side along Huai Hai Lu.

When they had nearly reached downtown, Lao Li signaled for Anna to pull over into a vast square lined with long gray buildings. They parked their bikes in the crowded rack and walked to the building on the right, from which hung a long red banner covered in huge black Chinese characters. Anna looked at Lao Li for a clue, but he just beckoned her to follow him.

Inside the foyer, Anna realized they were in an immense gallery. Lao Li led her up the stairs, where the rumbling of voices grew louder as they reached the top floor. A crowd of people

167

had gathered, many of them foreigners, along with a Chinese television crew. Anna skirted the crowd and saw students from her college who smiled at her. As she moved through the sweaty bodies, trying to see what they were all looking at, she came face to face with Laurent.

"Hey," he said, pushing Anna in front of him. "Look at this! Your boyfriend's putting on quite a show!"

Anna peered in and gasped. On an old school chair sat Chenxi, bare-chested. There was writing on the floor in front of him, but it was in Chinese. Slowly shaving off Chenxi's long hair with an antique razor blade was Old Wolf. He stood behind Chenxi, dressed in a white fabric cloak printed with Chinese news clippings. All over the cloak were handprints of blood-red paint. As another lock of hair dropped to the floor, Old Wolf shouted out some words. Anna stood mesmerized, trying to understand. People and cameras were pushing to get a view. Anna wanted to catch a glimpse of Chenxi's face but his head was bowed low onto his chest. On the floor around him, his blue-black hair glinted under the neon lights. Ebony strokes on the white stone tiles like Chinese characters on rice paper.

As the last lock of hair fell to the ground somebody cried out, as if in pain. Chenxi looked up, wild-eyed, and for a split second his gaze met Anna's. Before she knew what was happening he had darted out of the circle and was swallowed up by the crowd. When she looked back Old Wolf, too, had disappeared.

Anna struggled through the mass of bodies to the stairwell, hoping to find Chenxi. As she pounded down the empty staircase, she heard footsteps echoing her own, close behind.

In the foyer Laurent caught up with her and grabbed her by the arm.

"Let go! Let go!" she snarled, twisting out of his grip.

"No, you let go!" Laurent hissed. "Anna. You have to let him go."

LAO LI AND LAURENT WHEELED THEIR BIKES side by side along Huai Hai Lu, Anna a little way behind them. The two men had been talking earnestly for some time, but now Lao Li stepped onto the pedal of his bike and waved to both of them as he disappeared into the crowds.

Anna caught up to Laurent, impatient for news. "So that's where he's been, all this week?"

"I suppose so." Laurent paused to light a cigarette. Anna waited, irritable. He blew out a stream of smoke. "That exhibition was the work of a group of artists who call themselves The Red Wolves. Lao Li is one of them, Chenxi is their leader. The exhibition would have taken a lot of organization even though it's only on for one day. So, yes, that's probably where he's been all week."

"Why only one day?"

Laurent began to push his bike forward and Anna hurried to catch up. "Because it's extremely controversial. I don't know if you got a chance to look at the works, but some of them were very...um...how could you say? Political. To say the least. Did you see that big painting of the Chinese Statue of Liberty with a gag around her mouth? That was Lao Li's work. There were other paintings from students at your art college, too. They were all pieces about freedom of speech and democracy in China. Chenxi having his head shaved was the climax. You couldn't understand the characters on the floor in front of him, I suppose, but they said: 'I am having my head shaved for democracy.' These artists are hoping to get some foreign press.

"In Beijing, students are holding protests for democracy in Tiananmen Square. Chenxi and Old Wolf disappeared because someone called out that the police were on their way. You get into a lot of trouble doing that kind of thing here in China. Especially if foreign journalists are involved. I told you, Anna. Chenxi is trouble. You should stay away from him."

Anna stared at Laurent. "So why were you there? What do you care about Chenxi?"

"I don't. I ran into Lao Li at the noodle shop. He told me about it. I'm not interested in Chenxi, Anna. I only came because I thought you would probably be there. I came to warn you."

"Has my dad set you up for this?" Anna asked. "Is that what this is?"

"No! I know you might not think much of me, but I'm trying to look after you. There are a lot of things you don't understand about China." He paused and looked into her face. "Anna…"

"I can look after myself," Anna interrupted and pushed her bike forward. She didn't want to embarrass them both by hearing Laurent declare feelings for her. Her cheeks began to burn under Laurent's intense gaze and she looked around for a way to change the topic. They were walking beside a high brick wall. Anna peered into a long glass case that ran along it. Behind the dusty glass were rows of black-and-white photographs of faces. Mainly of young men with mug-shot stares.

"What are these?" Anna said. There was nothing Laurent liked better than to display his knowledge. It would get him talking about something else even though she really didn't want to listen. He annoyed her but, other than Chenxi and her father, he was the only person in Shanghai she could talk to in English. Once again she felt helpless. Always dependent on somebody to translate for her and help her around this indecipherable city.

Laurent read the Chinese characters below the photographs. "Look," he said, wheeling his bike to a poster farther along.

The photograph was blurry, but it was possible to make out a group of people standing around a man lying in the dust. His hands were tied behind his back and in front of him lay his decapitated head.

"See. That's what happens to criminals here," Laurent said, pointing to the photographs.

Anna shuddered. "What did they do?"

"Mostly drug dealers."

She looked at him. "Doesn't that worry you?" She pointed at the headless man in the photograph.

"Me?" Laurent gasped. "I don't deal drugs!"

"You sell hashish."

"That's just to people at the university. I don't sell to make money, or anything. You're mad."

Anna raised her eyebrows and shrugged. "Maybe?" She skirted her bike into the traffic, glad to be rid of him.

ANNA WATCHED HER FATHER help himself to the salad, and stared distractedly at the other tables. They had come to the restaurant where they had talks. Her procrastinating time was over.

A waiter in a bow tie stood in a corner cleaning his ears with a matchstick. Anna smiled. She was beginning to admire the Chinese. They were conformists perhaps, from a Western point of view, but they were also remarkably nonconformist as individuals. Chenxi's exhibition had moved her. *That* must be true freedom of expression, she thought. *That* was something powerful. Chenxi was right. It would mean nothing to shave your head in an art gallery in the U.S. In China it was pure defiance!

She was desperate to see him again. If only she hadn't been so spoiled and naïve! She would prove to him that she wasn't merely an ignorant foreigner. She could learn. The adage was true: the more you know, the more you realize you don't know. Chenxi had so much to teach her. If only she had been willing to learn, been less narrowminded and obstinate… She still had time to make up for it. Her father was offering her that time. Giving up her art to study alongside that pompous Laurent was only a small sacrifice to make for being with Chenxi. This was meant to be. The problem had been resolved of its own accord. Once again, Anna had been able to leave the decision in the hands of fate.

"Dad, I've decided to take up your offer to drop art and stay on for a year in Shanghai to study Chinese. I think you are right. It would be a great learning opportunity for me."

Mr. White almost choked. "Well, Anna. I must say I thought I'd have to make up your mind for you again. That's wonderful news! I'll look into organizing it right away. And I'm sure our friend Laurent will be able to help."

Anna picked at her pasta. Mr. White ordered another bottle of wine from the clean-eared waiter.

Anna and her father went by taxi to the art college the next morning. Keen to get his daughter back on the right track, he insisted on arranging everything immediately. Before she could change her mind, Mr. White fixed things up with the disappointed director, who had been hoping Anna might have stayed longer. Her special foreigner's school fees had already bought him a color television.

"She no like our college? Chenxi not good translator?"

While Mr. White wrote him a consoling check for the remaining amount due, Anna went to her classroom to retrieve her "Four Treasures" and speak to Chenxi.

To her dismay, he was not there. Anna gazed longingly at his desk, as if she could make him materialize just by visualizing him. As she rolled her brushes into their straw mat, she tried to catch Lao Li's attention to ask where he was. Strangely, none of the students had looked up from their work as Anna walked in.

"Psst! Psst! Lao Li!" she whispered.

The teacher was watching them. Lao Li glanced over. He shook his head, pleading with his eyes for her not to draw attention to him.

Anna wrapped her ink stone in newspaper and placed it in her backpack, stalling for time. From the corridor echoed the booming voice of her father, and the whining of the director's secretary. Their heads appeared in the doorway.

"Come on, Anna," Mr. White said briskly. "The taxi's waiting downstairs!"

Anna swung her bag on her back and walked toward her father. As she reached the door she glanced back at Lao Li. He made a furtive gesture of eating noodles before bowing his head again. Anna, relieved, turned to walk out of the classroom.

ANNA AND HER FATHER CROSSED SUZHOU CREEK in the taxi, heading toward the university where she would begin her study of Chinese. As they wound up their windows, Anna looked out at the houseboats clustered like open sores under the bridge. A child smeared in soot stared up at the taxi, before he scampered off along the slimy riverbank.

Anna imagined the days ahead, crossing back over this bridge to meet Chenxi, learning to speak enough Mandarin at the university to become independent. Her growing reliance on Laurent as her guide and translator was something she was desperate to get rid of. He was already more interested in her than was comfortable, yet she still needed him too much to ditch him. She reassured herself that he was only interested in her because her father offered him good business opportunities in China, and Mr. White loved Laurent because he kept his daughter in line. So, it was a plan that worked for everyone, wasn't it? Anna clutched her backpack on her lap and conjured up a vision of Chenxi.

After they had filled in forms and Mr. White had paid the deposit, the dean showed Anna how to find the beginners' class and invited her to come along the next day to a special Saturday morning class. He explained that she had already missed a few weeks and would have quite a lot of catching up to do. Mr. White looked concerned and Anna promised them both she would study hard. And she would. She had no intention of learning Mandarin to do business in China, but rather to escape the shackles of Laurent and find her way to Chenxi.

When she peeked into the classroom, Anna was surprised to see students of so many different nationalities. She had forgotten during her stay in China that foreigners came in colors other than white. The dean introduced Anna to the teacher and they walked on.

"Will you be staying here at the university?" the dean asked Anna. "Or with your father?"

"At the university."

"With my father."

 They both answered at once.

 Mr. White looked confused.

"I could study so much better in your apartment, Dad," Anna

explained. "Laurent told me that here at the university they never stop having parties!" Anna didn't like the idea of living in the same building as Laurent and she knew it would be easier to see Chenxi in private if she didn't have to share a dorm room with another student.

"It's true." The dean shook his head. "This year's students seem to be particularly rowdy."

Mr. White pondered the issue. "Well. OK. We'll see how it goes." It unnerved him when his plans weren't followed to the letter. "Well, it looks like everything's settled, so I'd better get to work. I've arranged for Anna to meet the French student, Laurent, for lunch," he explained to the dean.

"It is good she has made some friends," the dean nodded. "I know Laurent. His Mandarin is excellent."

The dean shook hands with Mr. White and excused himself. Anna and her father walked out of the school to where the taxi was waiting at the front entrance.

"Well, shall we get your bike out of the trunk then? You sure you're all right to ride back on your own? You'll know the way?"

"Yes, Dad. We're only over the bridge from the art college. I've ridden this way every day for the last four weeks!"

Mr. White pressed some FEC into Anna's palm. "Just in case. OK, I'll see you tonight then, dear."

"I'll be fine, Dad," said Anna guiding him toward the car door.

She watched the taxi ease into the flow of traffic and then walked her bike back to the entrance of the university to wait for Laurent. She didn't have to wait long. He wheeled his bike around the corner and, when he saw Anna, he grinned and waved.

"Hey! Thought I might take you somewhere nice for lunch instead of that greasy old noodle stall."

Anna panicked, remembering her plan to meet Lao Li. "No, no, we have to go to the noodle shop."

"Why?"

"I want to. I really feel like noodles. Come on. Please?" She felt embarrassed to watch him soften under her pleading. He agreed and they rode their bikes back over the bridge.

Minutes later, they sat opposite each other at one of the grubby tables in the crowded restaurant. Anna had let Laurent try to be gallant: he ordered and paid for her food. They now sat in silence while the boiling soup cooled. Anna watched the entrance behind him for any sign of Lao Li.

"It's great news that you will be studying with me at the university," Laurent began.

"Don't get the wrong idea, Laurent." Anna scowled. "I'm not doing it to be with you!" She gobbled her noodles, hoping to make herself as unattractive as possible. After chewing on a gristly piece of dried meat she cleared her throat and spat it to the floor.

Laurent rolled his eyes. "Picking up Chinese habits quickly, aren't you?"

Anna looked up and saw Lao Li edging his way in. She beckoned him over. There were no stools left so he crouched at the table. Anna saw his eyes flit back and forth as Laurent and he shook hands. Lao Li spoke to Laurent in Chinese and, a moment later, stood and left the shop.

"What did he say?" Anna said to Laurent. "Did he talk to you about Chenxi?"

Laurent sneered. "So, that's why you wanted to come here? I'm your messenger boy now, am I? Well, Lao Li said to tell you that Chenxi has gone into hiding. He said you mustn't try to make contact with him. Chenxi is in trouble with the police. They know Lao Li is Chenxi's friend so you must stay away from him, or he'll be in trouble, too!" He leaned back on his stool. "Ha! I told you, didn't I?"

Anna pushed her bowl of noodles away. She wanted to be sick. She glared at Laurent. "If you're lying, or even exaggerating, you bastard, I'll kill you!"

"Would I lie to you?" Laurent mocked.

"Fuck off!" snapped Anna. Her mind was in a whirl. The stench of the noodle shop was too much for her. She jumped up from the table and charged outside.

"See you at school!" Laurent called out in a singsong voice.

She despised him.

ANNA RODE FAST. She pushed down hard on the pedals until her muscles ached and her forehead streamed with sweat. Inside she screamed. She rode faster, faster, until in a flash the bike slid out from under her and she found herself skidding along the asphalt. The heat seared through her skin to the bone. She lay still. The roar of the traffic came from far away.

"*Ooh, wai guo ren!*" said a gentle voice. Anna looked up. Around her, in minutes, a circle of people had formed, maybe fifty of them. All staring down openmouthed at the blood and gravel that clung to Anna's knees.

"You see!" Anna screamed at them, salty tears stinging the wound on her chin. "Foreigners bleed, too!"

24

Too stiff and sore even to walk, Anna lay in bed for a week, grappling with the Chinese exercises her new teacher had sent home for her. Another week slipped by but she refused to leave the apartment. The wounds were healing, she had no broken bones, but she would not look in the mirror for fear of the scabs she would see.

By the third week, the wounds had softened into buckled pink scars. The face in the mirror reflected only shades of yellow and gray. She could have gone to the university, but now she felt sick. Nauseous. Most mornings she woke up with a roaring appetite but, after a bowl of cereal, promptly threw it up. Anna tried to tell herself it was a tummy bug, but when her breasts began to ache, and her period was two weeks overdue, she began to worry. Could she be pregnant? She cursed herself for having taken a risk, but she thought it had only been days after her period had finished. Perhaps she had got the dates wrong?

She had to find out, but there was nothing in her useless Chinese textbooks about pregnancy tests or abortions. She wouldn't know how to find her way to a hospital, let alone understand what they were saying to her.

Several times she had tried ringing the art college to see if Chenxi had returned but they were always elusive and Lao Li would never come to the phone. If only she could speak to Chenxi. This wasn't something she should be doing on her own. After all, he was the father. Father! The idea of it panicked and thrilled her. Would he want to be a father? More importantly, did she want to be a mother? At eighteen!

She thought about the words of the old fortune-teller at Fuxing Park. Had he been right? Was this her destiny? She lay back on the bed and poked at her belly. Was something really growing in there? The possibility was terrifying. She thought of calling a friend back home, but her old school friends seemed a world away now and, to be honest, she didn't really want them knowing. Two girls at her school had gotten pregnant that she knew of and, even though each had chosen a different outcome, their reputations had been equally tarnished.

She didn't want to worry her mother before she knew for sure. And there was no way she was telling her father. Besides, it was still possible that it might all be in her head.

There was only one person she knew in Shanghai who could help her. Picking up the telephone, she dialed the university and waited while they searched for Laurent at the other end. The thought of asking him for help made her skin crawl, but she had no choice. And, if she was pregnant, she had to make a decision right away.

"You took your time," Anna snapped when Laurent arrived at the apartment. "Come on, let's go. My father will be home after lunch."

"Well, it looks like my warnings about not getting involved with Chenxi came too late," Laurent said with a smile as they got into the elevator. "Assuming that Chenxi is the man involved here?"

Anna fumed. She had guessed she was going to have to put up with a fair amount of crap, but had hoped that he might find a grain of empathy for her situation. "Do you think you could avoid lecturing me just for today? I asked for help, not advice, OK? And, really, this has nothing to do with you."

"You might not even be pregnant, you know," Laurent suggested.

"Look, I may only be a woman," said Anna, "but as a woman give me credit for having expertise in at least one area that you don't!"

The elevator doors opened and Anna walked out first. "Ooh, pregnancy doesn't suit you!" Laurent murmured into her back.

In angry silence they rode their bikes side by side all the way to the Shanghai Number One Women's Hospital.

At the entrance Laurent grabbed Anna's hand for a moment.

"Please, Anna," he said.

She turned around to face him.

"Don't decide anything today, will you? I mean about an abortion, if that's what you want." He looked away, reddening. "I had a Spanish girlfriend two years ago who got pregnant. She had an abortion here and they really messed her up. Not just physically but emotionally too. She can't have babies anymore. It's the one-child policy thing. The doctors are just taught to take everything out to stop women falling pregnant again. I wouldn't want that to happen to you. It would be better to get it done in the U.S. Just go for a test here. Find out how far along you are. Pretend to them you want to keep the baby. Just for today, OK? You can always come back later if you change your mind."

Anna stared at Laurent. She nodded, unexpectedly touched by his concern, and he turned away, embarrassed.

A woman peered out from her sentry box at the entrance to the hospital. She was passing out different tickets that allowed new arrivals access to the correct buildings. "*Ni yao bu yao? Do you want it or not?*" she said to Laurent and Anna.

"She wants it," Laurent replied.

The woman handed Anna a yellow ticket. "Want it. Number two building. That one over there. Go inside and line up at the first window to pay."

Anna walked with Laurent past the bright peony bed to the stained gray building. The flowers were kept by an old man who hovered with a rake, guarding them from harm. He stared at the foreigners as they passed.

"*Ni yao bu yao?* Want it or not?" the nurse behind the desk asked. She wore a grimy white coat and a blue plastic shower cap on her head. A white tin bowl with a few rice grains glued to the greasy bottom was staining the papers beneath it. The woman behind Anna in the queue strained to see over her shoulder, to look at the foreigners, to discover if they could speak Chinese and what they would say.

"She wants it."

"How old is she?" the nurse barked at Laurent.

Laurent asked Anna.

She replied, "Eighteen."

Laurent looked surprised.

"*Aiya!* She's too young! She's just a baby herself!"

Laurent translated to Anna who retorted, "No I'm not! Plenty of people have them at my age."

The nurse shook her head as she counted out the money and handed Anna a clear plastic ticket with red Chinese characters on it.

"Go and wait in that room there. Keep your ticket and hand it to the doctor."

There was no space left in the waiting room. Row upon row of wooden benches were filled; people were squatting in corners and one man lay on the floor asleep. It was more like a waiting room at the train station than at a hospital.

A woman cleared her throat and spat, another shouted at a restless child. A dozing man with his feet up on a seat grumbled and swung his legs to the floor to let Anna and Laurent sit down. The woman sitting in front muttered at him. He snarled and slunk off to find another seat. Seeing her chance, the woman slipped in next to Anna, beaming.

"Hello!" she said, turning to Anna. "Do you speak English?"

"No," Laurent replied, in Chinese, not wanting to be bothered with all of her questions.

Anna felt sick again and remembered the three spots of blood she had discovered in her underpants the previous morning. Not exactly a period, but perhaps she wouldn't have to make a decision after all? Was she even entitled to make that decision without consulting Chenxi? She would have to find him. This was too important to heed Lao Li's warnings. Lao Li would have to tell her where he was. She needed to see him.

There were spots of blood on the wall in the waiting room at Shanghai Number One Women's Hospital. Not carmine red like those on Anna's underpants, but rust-colored and smudged. She remembered an exhibition in San Francisco where the artist had painted an enormous canvas with pig's blood and beside his painting ran a video of the sacrifice. It was gory stuff, but the artist insisted from his video, over the squeals of the beast, that it was art. Sensual. A religious experience. The audience around her had gasped, offended. Did that artist know that all the walls of the Forbidden City were painted in pig's blood? She smiled: the Chinese government would probably have been less offended by the sacrifice of a pig than by Chenxi's haircut.

On wet days when she walked through the food market near the art college, the street flowed with blood. And at the Muslim restaurant where Chenxi had taken her to eat mutton dumplings, a sheep's head looked on from a corner, the blood dripping from its open neck. She thought about the delicious soup she had sipped, made from blocks of liver-colored congealed blood, and the grinning butchers with blood-stained hands who shooed flies from the hunks of beef solidifying in the sun.

In such a short while she had become accustomed to the sight of blood. In China, it was just a part of life that Americans managed to avoid in their sanitized, cling-wrapped supermarket existence. Yet now, the sight of those three spots of blood on her underpants could signify life and death so much more than any other blood she had seen.

Anna wished Chenxi was sitting beside her rather than Laurent. What would he think? Would he want to keep it? She had no idea. She hardly knew him.

25

After three or four minutes a nurse came out and called her name. Anna gave her the ticket. Everyone in the waiting room knew that, as a foreigner, Anna would be seen first. Nobody complained.

"Would you come with me?" she asked Laurent. "To translate?" She didn't want to admit that she found his company reassuring.

Laurent asked the nurse if he could accompany Anna. She blushed and said she'd have to ask the doctor. Usually this was women's business. "I'll have to pretend I'm your husband," Laurent explained to Anna.

The doctor came out and ushered Laurent and Anna into a small empty office. She sat down behind a glass-topped desk and motioned for them to take the two chairs in front.

"Now," she began in excellent English, as she wrote some Chinese characters at the top of a form, "Do you want it or not?"

188

"We want it," Laurent said.

Anna blushed.

The nurse frowned, turning to Anna once again. "How old are you?"

"Eighteen."

"Hmm…" She filled in the appropriate box and her pen moved to the next question. "When was your period due?"

"Two weeks ago."

"Oh. Are your periods normally regular?"

"Yes. Very," Anna said.

The doctor continued. "Are you married?"

"Yes," she lied, not looking at Laurent. She knew this was a big deal in China.

"Any problems? Pain?"

"Not really. Though I did find some blood in my underpants yesterday."

Laurent looked at Anna.

"Mmm… It could have been a light period, although sometimes in pregnancy you can still have some spotting. You also want to be sure that it's not a threatened miscarriage."

Anna didn't answer.

"We'll have to examine you and run some tests. It's the room across the hall, but I'm afraid your husband can't go with you. It's a room for women only."

The doctor led Anna across the waiting room and pointed her in the right direction. Laurent sat down to wait.

THE EXAMINING ROOM HAD FOUR NARROW BEDS covered with dirty white sheets that were slipping off the green plastic mattresses. There were two desks in a corner and plenty of people milling around. Some wore white coats and rubber gloves; others were in ordinary clothes.

Anna was led to one of the middle beds and three Chinese women were taken to the remaining ones. She hoisted herself up and lay down.

A nurse came over and directed her to take off her jeans and underpants and to put her feet into the stirrups that hung above the bed.

She undressed self-consciously while the nurse waited. Then she slipped a paper towel under Anna's buttocks.

Everyone in the room seemed to be staring at her. She closed her eyes, trying to shut out her humiliation. The nurse touched Anna's head. "Very pretty hair."

A doctor walked over with a swab and some tissues. She snapped on some gloves and inserted two fingers into Anna's vagina. Anna winced. She couldn't believe she had thought she'd only need to pee into a specimen jar.

The doctor then did the same with the swab. When she extracted the swab everyone in the room, except Anna, seemed fascinated by the little lump of pale pink on the end. The nurse gave Anna a tissue to wipe herself then signaled for her to get dressed; the next woman was already by the side of the bed, waiting to get up.

As she left the examining room Anna was handed a glass slide with a pinkish smear on it. Laurent hurried up to her.

"Are you all right?" he asked. "You look very pale."

"I'm not used to being examined in a room full of strangers."

"The Chinese have no sense of privacy," Laurent frowned. "What now?" he asked, looking at the slide in Anna's hand. Anna shrugged, so Laurent took her arm and led her down the stairs, where the other women from the examining room were heading.

On the lower floor, Anna followed a group of women with slides in their hands to a bustling crowd around a little desk.

She stood on the outside of the group to wait her turn. A woman from behind bumped her in the back and another tried to squeeze in front of her. Two women were arguing about who should go first. There were about twenty women, all scrabbling for attention. The nurse behind the desk took her time filling out the stickers to label the slides while the crowd jostled to be the next in line.

When Anna was bumped again, she swore and almost dropped her precious slide. She squeezed the glass hoping it wouldn't crack. Anyone would think we were livestock, not people, she grumbled to herself.

"And so?" Laurent asked when Anna eventually surfaced, slide deposited.

"I don't know."

"What did the doctor say?"

"I can't remember." She felt close to tears.

"What?"

"I don't know what to do. I can't understand anything they say!" Anna blurted.

"Come on. You're hopeless. We'll go and find that first doctor again, the one who spoke English."

Laurent strode back up the stairs and Anna followed, grateful again that he had taken control.

In the small office the doctor was eating her lunch and she wasn't pleased to see the foreigners. She glared out from behind the bowl while she scooped rice into her mouth.

"What is it?"

"Well, we don't know anything yet!" Laurent said.

"Come back tomorrow." She shooed them away with her chopsticks.

"We want to find out today!"

"It's not possible. Unless you have an ultrasound."

"She wants an ultrasound then!"

"It's not possible."

"Why?"

"It's very expensive."

"We'll pay."

"It's not possible! No, no! She needs to have drunk water all day and not gone to the toilet. She needs a full bladder to push it into view. Otherwise there's no use. You won't see anything."

"Can't we try?"

"I told you it's no use. Come back after lunch. Four o'clock. OK? It's on the sixth floor. After lunch. Or tomorrow." She returned to her rice bowl. Laurent led Anna out of the room. She knew already where they were headed.

IN THE CORRIDOR NEXT TO THE ULTRASOUND ROOM was a large urn. Anna squatted beside it with a jar of boiling water, blowing to cool it before she swallowed its scalding contents.

Laurent paced the empty corridor as she drank. Anna could hear the clicking of chopsticks and the chatter of nurses behind the closed door. After five jars in a row he asked, "Are you full?"

"I've burned my mouth."

"Are you full?"

"Yes."

"Come on then. One more."

Anna scowled, but did as she was told. Laurent knocked on the door.

The nurse glared at the foreigners and snapped at Laurent in Chinese. Anna listened to them arguing back and forth until eventually Laurent turned to her to explain.

"She wanted to see your ticket. I told her you'd lost it and that you really needed an ultrasound. She still didn't want to let us in so I told her we absolutely had to come today, that you were my wife and you were sick and that we'd traveled a really long distance to get here. Sheez! I feel like I'm bloody Joseph at the inn or something. I hope you're grateful!"

"I am," Anna said meekly. And she meant it. She had no idea how she would have managed without him that day, and the thought humbled her.

A nurse took Anna gently by the hand and pulled her into the ultrasound room. Laurent waited outside.

Anna was led to another bed. She lay down again. This room

was empty except for two smiling nurses. One whispered to the other while stroking Anna's forehead with her cool hands. While the other went to get the equipment, the first nurse played with Anna's hair. Anna closed her eyes and imagined she was lying on a clean hospital bed in San Francisco.

The nurse returned with a tube of jelly, which she squeezed onto Anna's abdomen. Then she pushed the ultrasound baton across it.

"Look. You see," she said.

Anna opened her eyes in dread. She hadn't been able to wish it away after all. On the blurry screen a small white shape pulsed in a sea of gray.

"What's that?" Anna asked.

"Baby," the nurse said.

Anna felt her heart surge.

26

The teahouse in the Yu Yuan Gardens seemed to grow out of the water lilies. Its ancient curving roof made from crumbling earth tiles was of the same swamp-green glaze as the water. The carved wooden window scenes were like the twisting stems of the lotuses. If it were not for the swarms of Chinese tourists posing on its bridges or haggling with the stall owners for soft drinks and film, you could sit drinking your green tea from the thimble-sized cups and be transported into another dynasty.

Laurent poured Anna some more tea. "The third infusion is the best, they say."

"Mmm?" said Anna, distracted. She preferred it when he didn't talk. During the ride to the teahouse he had paid her the courtesy of not talking. It was Anna's suggestion they come. She wasn't ready to go back to the apartment.

"Anna, don't get an abortion here. Get it done in the States.

It's safer. You wouldn't even have to tell Chenxi. Nobody would know."

Anna took an angry sip. She wanted to scream. "Why is it that everyone seems to feel they have the right to tell me what to do all the time? Do I have a sign pinned on my back that says 'I'm a Stupid Little Girl—Please Tell Me What to Do?' What if I decide to keep the baby? Huh? What if I decide to keep Chenxi's baby and we get married and I bring him to America and we live happily ever after? That would piss you off, wouldn't it?"

Laurent shook his head. "You don't need a sign on your back. It comes right out of your mouth. You are sheltered and naïve. You just can't get that fairy tale out of your head, can you? Do I have to spell it out? Let him go! Forget him! Don't you understand? You're already in enough trouble. So is he."

"Why? So I can come running to you? Not in my lifetime!" She aimed the dart well. Laurent blanched and looked down into his tea. "The only person I want to stay away from is you!" Anna stood up, knocking over the cup. A dribble of tea seeped into Laurent's pants as he watched her force her way out of the crowded teahouse.

ANNA'S FATHER WAS HOME when she arrived at the apartment. She could see from his grim face that something was wrong. She tried to sneak past him into her room.

"Where have you been?"

Anna sighed. "Drinking tea."

"Don't get smart with me, young lady. If you're well enough to be leaving this apartment you're well enough to be going to university. I rang today, and your teacher told me you haven't handed in any of the assignments she posted to you. I've had just about enough of this fooling around, Anna. You assured me that you would study Chinese. Once again you've let me down. You are letting your life slip away. Wasting your opportunities. You're not a foolish schoolgirl any more. It's time to grow up now, and start doing some serious work!"

Anna felt an unfamiliar sensation rising inside her. Floating up and fizzing in her head. Words were being formed in her mouth. Words that, once out, could never be retrieved. She faced her father. "You know what, Dad? You're right."

Mr. White stared at his daughter.

"It *is* time I took my life into my own hands. Time I made my own decisions. You know what? I've decided I'm not going to be a businesswoman, or a doctor, or an engineer. I'm going to be an artist, after all."

"Don't be ridiculous!"

"I'm going to drop out of university, college, school, whatever, live on my own, paint, and you know what else?" Anna continued giddily. "I'm pregnant!"

It was out. A sense of lightness overcame her—she had told the truth to her father. She stared at him, defiant.

Mr. White's mouth fell open. "You're joking." He shook his head. "Laurent?"

A smile curled on Anna's lips at the thought of her final triumph. "No!" she pronounced. "Chenxi!"

This revelation was too much. In an instant, Anna saw all her father's hopes for her erased. Over his face descended a weary mask. "You stupid girl. You're not going to keep it, are you?"

"I don't think that has anything to do with you, Dad."

"What a waste," he sighed, shaking his head. "Just like your mother—a waste of an intelligent brain! If that is how you want to be, if you think you're old enough to be making these kind of decisions, then you are on your own. You'd better ring your mother, I would say, and hope to God that she will take you back, because you're not staying here." With that, he stormed out of the room.

Anna went to her bedroom, shaking. She stared out of the window. She felt the sickening sensation of the ground dropping away beneath her feet. From now on, everything was up to her. She was on her own. Was this what it felt like to be free?

In Fuxing Park an old man hugged a tree.

27

Anna spent the following day packing up her room. Now that she had declared herself out of his hands, Mr. White refused to have Anna stay with him another day. She was booked onto the first flight back to San Francisco. If she wanted to be independent and impulsive then she was on her own.

Anna's mother had been surprisingly calm and sympathetic. Perhaps now that her daughter's problems were bigger than her own it would give her a new role to play? She managed to persuade her tearful daughter over the phone that, whatever her decision, she would be better to act on it in the U.S. Besides, without her father's financial support, Anna couldn't afford to stay in China. She called the art college to speak to Chenxi, but once again got nowhere. "Chenxi no here," she was told, and when she asked to speak to Lao Li, he was always busy.

"Can you tell him to call me, please?" Anna insisted. "Can you tell him it's urgent? I know you have Chenxi's contact details there, his mother's address. Can you give her a message to tell him to call me? She'll know where he is."

The secretary assured Anna she would do her best and Anna waited indoors all day for the phone to ring. As she folded her clothes, it was easy to forget about the baby growing inside her. To avoid thinking about making a decision.

In the late afternoon, the phone rang.

"Chenxi?" she asked. It had to be.

"No, it's Laurent."

"Hello, Laurent." Her voice was cold.

"Anna," he said. He sounded out of breath. "I'm downstairs. Meet me in the park by the statue." Then he hung up.

Anna slammed down the phone. Laurent was the last person she felt like seeing, but perhaps he had news of Chenxi? She pulled on her sandals. Now that it was the end of May, the weather was becoming hotter every day. Anna allowed herself to feel pleased that she wouldn't be in Shanghai for the summer.

LAURENT STOOD WAITING, his back against the foot of the enormous statue. Towering over him, Marx and Engels discussed the state of communism in China. As Anna approached she saw that Laurent was even paler than usual. His shaved hair had begun to grow back and there was a dark bristle over his scalp. His skin was gray and his eyes were yellow. He looked grubby. Knowing that she was leaving, Anna could almost feel sorry for him.

Laurent curled his lip. "I'm in deep shit because of you!"

"What's wrong?" Anna said, taken aback. She had been ready to make amends.

"Thanks to you I've just spent all of today being interrogated by the police. I've written three letters of self-criticism, and I am about to be deported! Thanks to you, my future is fucked!" He prodded her in the shoulder with a bony finger.

"What are you talking about?" Anna snapped back. "Look, if you're talking about getting caught dealing hashish, that's nothing to do with me. You had it coming to you!"

"Oh yeah?" Laurent shouted. "What's this then?" He reached inside his pocket and thrust a wad of papers into her hand. Anna recognized her handwriting. They were photocopies of her journal. She didn't understand what was going on.

"You're an idiot! I warned you, but you live in your own bloody clean-cut naïve world, thinking nothing can touch you." He was trembling with fury.

Anna turned the pages. Her writing looked childish. She had never noticed that before. "But this is my journal! How could the police possibly…"

"Your *aiyi*? The spy? Remember? Did you think only your father's engineering contracts would be useful to her? Don't you know, you fool? We are living in China, here. You should never write things down!"

She skimmed down the pages to where Laurent's name was underlined. Of course, it was always his name on the pages she had written about hashish. She kept turning, transfixed. "I can't believe it…"

Until one of the pages made her stop. Chenxi's name was circled here. As she turned the page she saw it circled again and again. An icy wave came over her and she found it difficult to breathe. She looked up blankly at Laurent. He saw what she had noticed.

"Let me tell you something, girl." He pulled Anna to him by her shirt and hissed into her ear, "I don't give a fuck about Chenxi. I used to think I gave a fuck about you, but now I know that you're just an ignorant little bitch! It's bad enough that you've caused trouble for them, but now, me, too! You're pathetic."

Laurent spat at the dirt by her feet and was gone.

Anna stood stunned, gazing at the papers. Chenxi's name grew bigger and bigger and the circle around it redder and redder. Red Chinese characters scuttled over her handwriting like poisonous spiders. Sobbing, she ran out of the park into the apartment compound and clambered onto her bike.

The route to the college had never seemed so long nor the streets so busy. Cyclists dawdled in front of her. Inside the hollow of Anna's chest a small moth fluttered.

As she flew down through the marketplace, she calmed at the sight of the high college gate. Chenxi would come with her to America now, she thought. She would bring him back to her peaceful country where he would be safe. Where he could still do his art. Where he would be free. In her mind she wrote the note that she would slip into his desk. She had it all worked out.

It was meant to be.

THE CLASSROOM WAS EMPTY. Chenxi's desk was gone. His books, his brushes, even the mound of cigarette butts and pumpkin seed husks that had gathered at his feet. There was no trace of him. His space had closed over, as if he had never existed.

28

The thick wad of paper, one hundred and sixty pages, slid into the envelope. Thirteen months later, and this was the last hope Anna held of finding him. Her story, his story, it had begun as a desperate sort of release, but when she put it all together…could she dare call it a novel?

Anna had returned to the United States at the end of May. A few days later, on June 4, she turned on the news to see that tanks had rolled through Tiananmen Square in Beijing, to disperse a collection of students protesting peacefully for democracy. She watched, horrified by images of the army moving into the square from several directions, firing randomly on the unarmed protesters. The news anchor announced that hundreds of people were killed in the massacre, many of them innocent bystanders. In the days that followed, as Anna scanned the newspapers, her stomach churning, reports emerged of troops searching university campuses for ringleaders, beating and killing those they suspected of coordinating the protests. Art colleges, known to cultivate rebellious thought, were singled out. Many students fled the country.

Anna rang the college repeatedly over the first few days, desperate for news of Chenxi, but the phone was never answered. Even her father was unable to explain to Anna what was happening in China, as the only news coverage he was able to access was CNN. The local Chinese media had been banned from covering the event. Like most of the foreigners in Shanghai and Beijing, he fled on an emergency flight arranged by the U.S. consulate back to California, and stayed until it was safe to return to China. They had been terrifying weeks for Anna but, like all tragedies, the troubles in China were soon forgotten by most people and replaced by other newsworthy events.

Now Anna hesitated before licking the stamp and fixing it to the top right corner. If her book was published, if it sold well, if it was translated, Chenxi might read it. If. It was a wild idea, but it was all she had left. She had to know. Nothing was worse than not knowing.

From the little silver snuffbox sitting on her desk, Anna pulled out a worn note. She unfolded the paper and read the words again, even though she knew them by heart. Each time she studied the note she searched for clues as if they might suddenly appear, but it remained as cryptic as when she had first received it over a year ago.

HeLLo ANNA,
I seeN oLd WoLF.
He TeLL Me I TeLL You do NoT WRiTe aGaiN. PLease.
OuR FRieND is FRee now.
YouR FRieND,
Lao Li.

Anna folded the paper and placed it back in the snuffbox. Then she sealed the brown envelope and kissed it for luck. As she stood, the package slipped from her hands and thudded onto the wooden floorboards. Startled, the baby in the bassinet by her side began to cry. She picked him up and laid his head against her chest.

Anna stroked her son's fuzzy black hair and rocked him until he fell back to sleep. Outside, a single gull careened against the sun-bleached sky. She looked up at the painting that hung over her desk. From a Chinese landscape, her face gazed back at her.

AFTERWORD

I was nineteen when I first started collecting ideas for *Chenxi and the Foreigner*. From 1989 to 1992 I lived in China, studying traditional Chinese painting. During my first year in Shanghai, I wrote down the details of my life in journal entries and short stories, knowing that photographs could never capture the experiences and emotions in the way that words could. But it wasn't until several years later, when I was living in France, that I began to work all these pieces into a novel.

Many of the experiences I had as an art student in Shanghai, as well as the people I met while I was studying there, inspired this story. I invented its main thread but Chenxi, in particular, is loosely based on a close friend of mine who is still a wonderful painter but is now living in Europe.

I finished the manuscript in 1997 and it was eventually published in 2002, but in a different form from the book you have just read. When I recently read that edition, for the first time in years, I could see that, as a young and inexperienced writer, I had been afraid of my readership. Not so much of the young adult readers themselves, but of their parents, teachers, and librarians, otherwise known as "the gatekeepers" among children's authors.

I remembered how I had cut out swear words, sex scenes, and unfamiliar Chinese politics from the original manuscript for fear of being blocked by those gatekeepers and never reaching my audience. I also worried at the time that, if my novel were too obviously political, I might stir up a discussion I wasn't brave enough to enter into at that age.

Now, I realize how compromised the first version of *Chenxi and the Foreigner* became through my own self-censoring, which is ironic given that this is a novel about artistic freedom. I also know, especially now that my oldest son is a teenager, that inquisitive teenage readers worldwide will always seek out for themselves those books that take risks.

It's not often that an author gets the opportunity to rewrite a book after it has already been published. I began to revise *Chenxi* with excitement and trepidation. With the encouragement of my publishers, I changed the name of the main character to allow myself to see her with fresh eyes, and even changed the key decision she has to make at the end of the novel. I decided to include everything: the sex, the swear words and, in particular, the politics.

When I was first writing *Chenxi* I did not feel confident to include anything about the terrible massacre in Tiananmen Square in Beijing on June 4, 1989, as it was still close to the event and, in China, still taboo. Even though I was friends with many of my fellow students, this was not something they felt comfortable discussing for fear of finding themselves in trouble with the government.

Nearly twenty years later, I decided to set my novel in the period leading up to the Tiananmen Square protests, as I had originally intended. This meant I had to change many details throughout and especially the ending, which now refers to the massacre. Hundreds, and possibly thousands, of people were killed, although, because of the government's tight control over the media, it is unlikely a precise number will ever be known.

In researching this new ending, I was shocked to discover that, unlike the Cultural Revolution, about which information can be freely accessed, the events surrounding June 4, 1989, have been edited from any media inside mainland China. This includes books, magazines, newspapers, and websites. The Chinese government has declared the June Fourth Incident a forbidden topic.

This doesn't mean, however, that the massacre is forgotten. Each year, on its anniversary, the government places Tiananmen Square under tight security to make sure that there can be no public mourning. Dissidents are placed under house arrest. But in Hong Kong, thousands gather for a candlelight vigil in Victoria Park to remember those killed and to demand that the families of the victims receive recognition and compensation.

In 2007, I returned to Shanghai with my family. In many ways, Shanghai today is unrecognizable as the city I once lived in. The dusty shops on Huai Hai Lu that once sold old-fashioned polyester slacks and plastic sandals have been transformed into shining department stores with ten-meter-high (nearly 33 feet high) television screens advertising Dior perfumes and Calvin Klein underwear. All the alleyways I used to ride along have been razed to make way for new businesses that are part of China's booming economy. Nobody who is anybody rides a bike anymore. How is it then that this country, modern in so many ways, can still be so resistant when it comes to freedom of speech? Sadly, because of the lack of this most basic right, many young adults in China will never know the truth about June 4, 1989.

Chenxi and the Foreigner is a tribute to the Shanghai I once knew. It is also a tribute to artists all over the world who dare to speak freely, no matter what their art form may be, and to those artists who live in places where speaking out could cost them their lives.

＝ ACKNOWLEDGMENTS ＝

AFTER NEARLY TWENTY YEARS and three editions of this novel, I think the time has finally come to thank my father for all the ways he has contributed to what you now hold in your hands. For the experience of having lived and traveled all over the world; for managing to find scraps of nature in some of the world's most populated cities, and then taking us to camp in them; for wanting the best for me, then having to watch me walk in the other direction anyway; for his vast knowledge of contemporary and historical China; for his ongoing fascination with, empathy for, and understanding of the Chinese people, and, most of all, for passing on his love affair with China to me.

ABOUT THE AUTHOR

SALLY RIPPIN WAS BORN IN DARWIN, AUSTRALIA, but spent much of her childhood in Southeast Asia. At nineteen she moved to China for three years to study traditional Chinese painting in Shanghai and Hangzhou. Now she lives in Melbourne, where she writes, illustrates, and teaches writing for children at RMIT University. She has had over twenty books published for children of all ages, many of them award-winning. For more information, visit www.sallyrippin.com.